™

ANNOYING ORANGE™

YAY! YOU BOUGHT OUR BOOK! *WE LOVE YOU!*

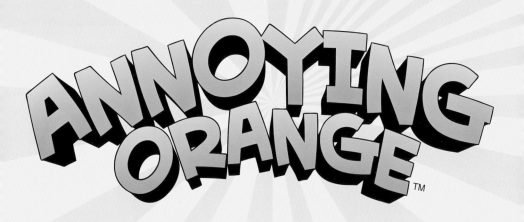

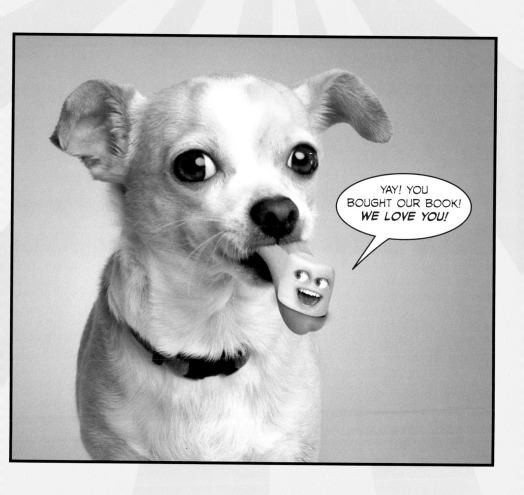

PAPERCUTZ™

PULPED FICTION

WHO THE HECK IS "ANN O. YING" AND HOW DID SHE GET *TOP BILLING?!*

Annoying Orange is created by DANE BOEDIGHEIMER

SCOTT SHAW! – Writer & Artist

MIKE KAZALEH – Writer & Artist

LAURIE E. SMITH – Colorist

PAPERCUTZ
NEW YORK

#3 "Pulped Fiction"
"Skipping Orange"
"Marshmallow Gets Down With its Peeps"
"The Story of Paul Onion"
"Nerville's Magna Carta"
Mike Kazaleh – Writer & Artist
Laurie E. Smith – Colorist
Tom Orzechowski – Letterer
"The Seed of Crime Fears Better Fruit-- Now with Extra Pulp!"
Scott Shaw! – Writer & Artist
Laurie E. Smith – Colorist
Janice Chiang – Letterer

Special thanks to: Gary Binkow, Tim Blankley, Dane Boedigheimer,
Spencer Grove, Teresa Harris, Reza Izad, Debra Joester, Polina Rey, Tom Sheppard, Grace Wen
Director of Marketing: Jesse Post
Production Coordinator: Beth Scorzato
Associate Editor: Michael Petranek
Jim Salicrup
Editor-in-Chief

ISBN: 978-1-59707-420-9 paperback edition
ISBN: 978-1-59707-421-6 hardcover edition

Printed in Canada
July 2013 by Friesens Printing
1 Printers Way
Altona, MB ROG OBO

Papercutz books may be purchased for business or promotional use.
For information on bulk purchases please contact Macmillan Corporate
and Premium Sales Department at (800) 221-7945 x5442.

Distributed by Macmillan
First Printing

MEET THE FRUIT...

CAN YOU TOUCH YOUR NOSE WITH YOUR TONGUE?

WHAT *NOSE?*

THE SHALLOT KNOWS!

ORANGE

Has success spoiled Orange (pictured above, right)? Has getting over a gazillion hits on his YouTube videos made him think he's better than other fruit, aside from Apple? Has starring in the hit Cartoon Network TV series gone to his head? And most importantly, with the humongous success of the ANNOYING ORANGE (pictured above, left) graphic novel series from Papercutz, has Orange become so celebrated, that his ego now dwarves the ego of every other star in Hollywood combined? Or has he miraculously remained unchanged? Is he still the same cute, sweet (sort of), yet annoying fruit his fans and friends have grown to love? We asked several of his friends for their opinions on this pressing issue...!

PEAR

We asked Pear "Has success spoiled Orange?" and after pondering for just a few moments, he slyly evaded the question by answering, "No! Orange is not spoiled at all! Nerville has done an excellent job of making sure each and every fruit at Daneboe's Supermarket is kept as fresh as possible. Orange spoiled? Of course not! He's as fresh as ever—just look at him!" Spoken like the true friend to Orange that Pear is known to be. When we explained that we didn't mean "spoiled" literally, Pear replied, "Well, then I literally don't know what you're talking about."

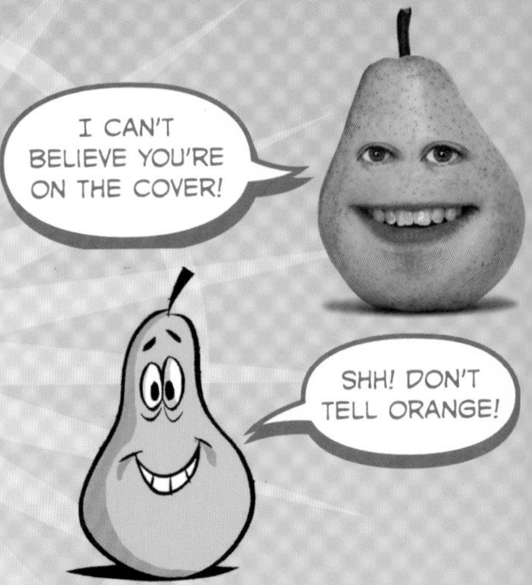
I CAN'T BELIEVE YOU'RE ON THE COVER!
SHH! DON'T TELL ORANGE!

MIDGET APPLE

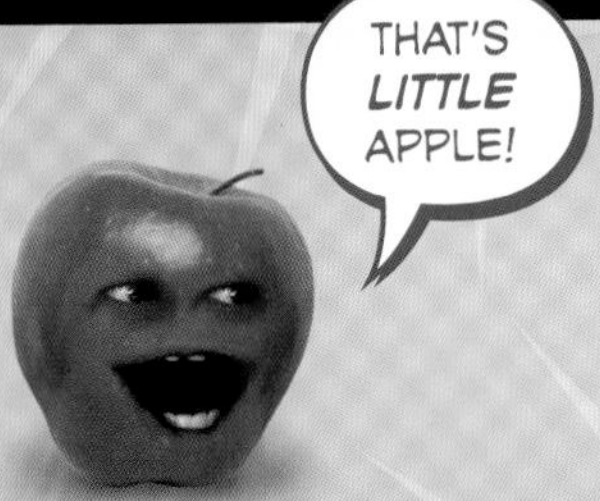
THAT'S *LITTLE* APPLE!

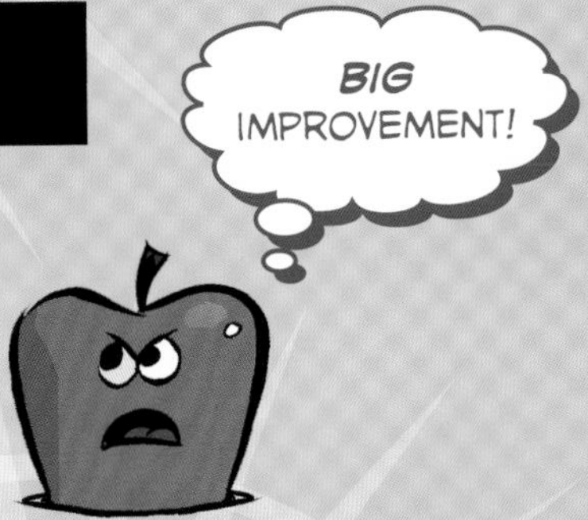
BIG IMPROVEMENT!

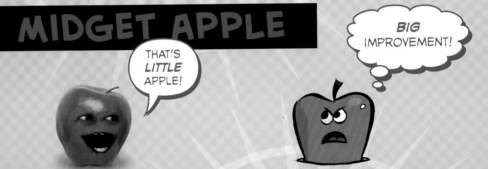

When we attempted to ask Midget Apple the same question, we didn't get very far. We started simply by saying, "Excuse us, Midget Apple—" and he quickly cut us off. "My name IS NOT Midget Apple! How many times must I tell everyone that?!" He then stormed off, leaving before we could even finish asking our question.

GRANDPA LEMON

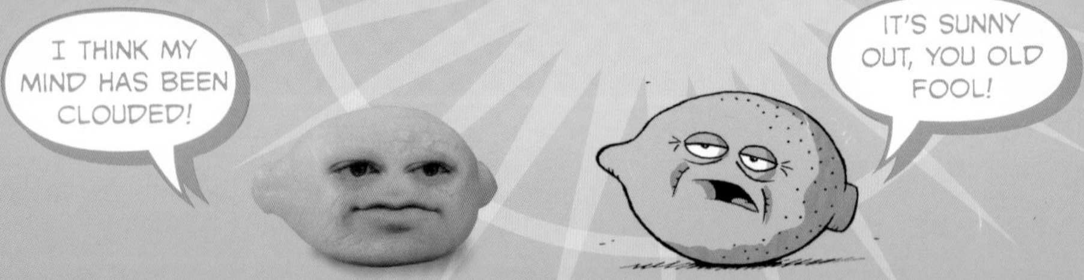
I THINK MY MIND HAS BEEN CLOUDED!
IT'S SUNNY OUT, YOU OLD FOOL!

We were beginning to suspect that Orange had tipped off all of his friends and asked them not to speak to us. Or if they did, not answer our question. For example, we asked Grandpa Lemon if he thought success spoiled Orange, and he replied, "Why would 'recess' spoil him? Everyone loves recess! That's when school's out!" We tried asking again, but before we could finish the question, the old fruit fell fast asleep.

PASSION FRUIT

WE'RE FRUITILICIOUS!

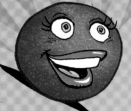

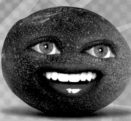

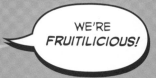

Passion Fruit was far more cooperative. When asked if success spoiled Orange, she quickly replied "Of course not! He has always been exactly the way he is—annoying, yet somewhat lovable despite himself. There's something about him that's irresistible, but I can't quite figure out what!"

MARSHMALLOW

I LOVE UNICORNS!
ME TOO! YAY!

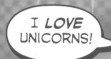

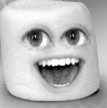

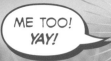

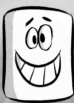

Marshmallow was willing to answer the question "Has success spoiled Orange?" But we're still trying to figure out Marshmallow's answer—"Orange is Orange! And Orange is one of the colors of the rainbow and I love rainbows! Yay! Answering questions is fun!"

GRAPEFRUIT

IF I WAS ANY MORE PUMPED-UP, I'D EXPLODE!
THAT WOULD BE ME ALL OVER!

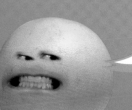

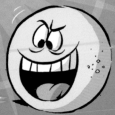

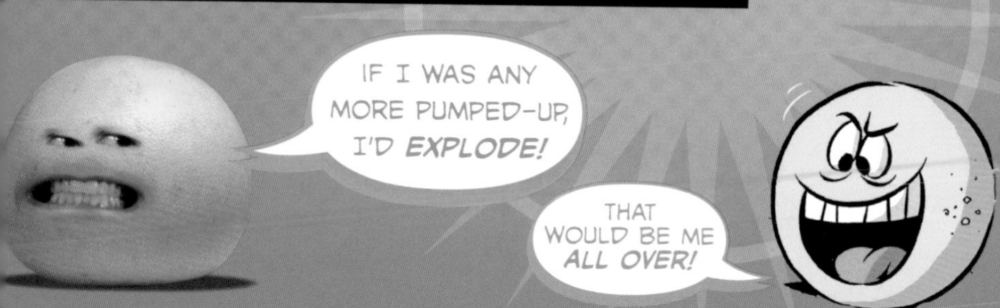

Finally, we asked Grapefruit, "Has success spoiled Orange?" Here's his answer: "What 'success'? Any success that's come that whiny little citrus' way has been due to me! The only reason anyone pays attention to his videos, TV show, or graphic novels is because they're hoping to get a glimpse of me! You know it's true!" With that, we simply gave up.

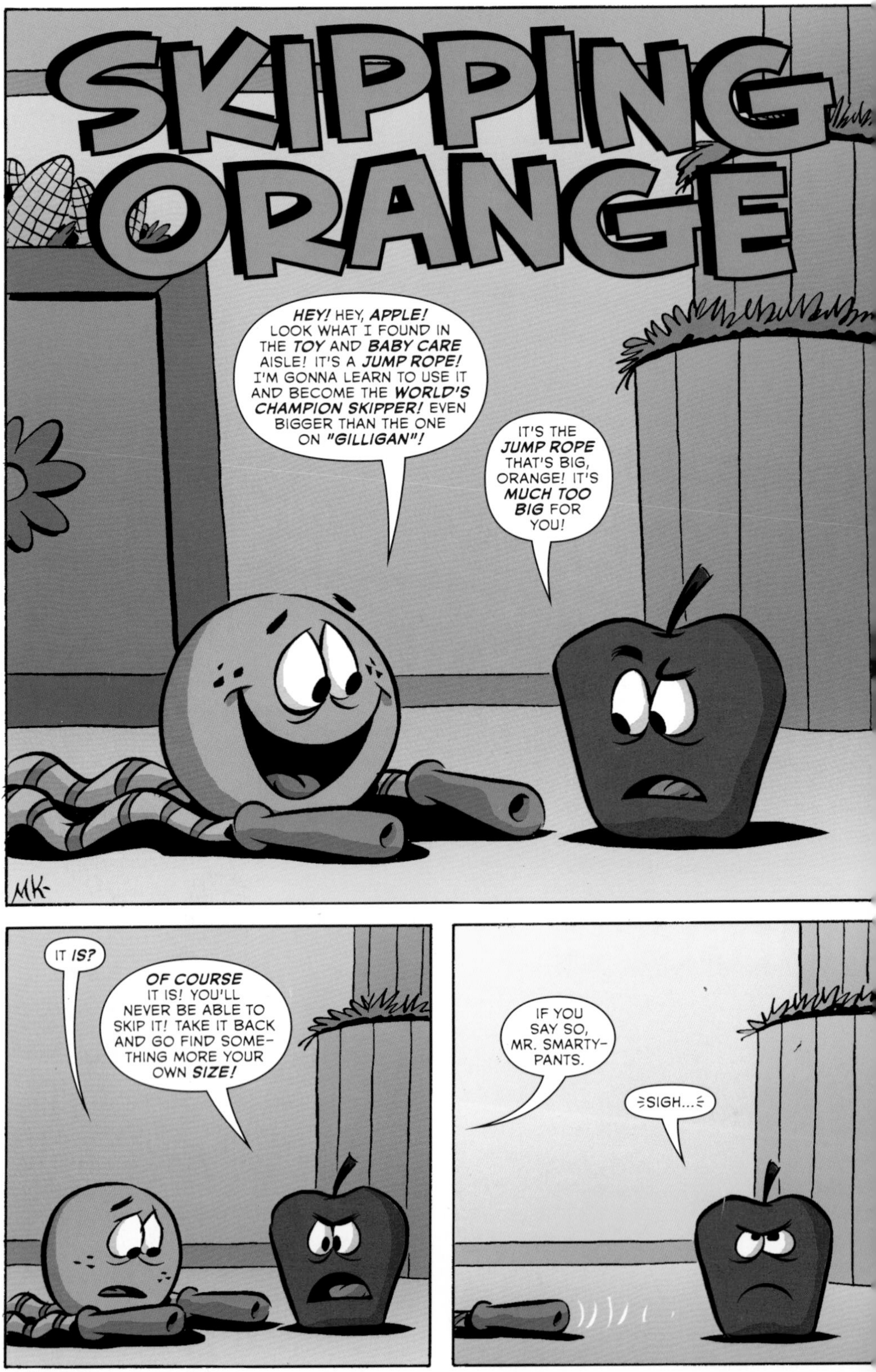
SKIPPING ORANGE
HEY! HEY, APPLE! LOOK WHAT I FOUND IN THE TOY AND BABY CARE AISLE! IT'S A JUMP ROPE! I'M GONNA LEARN TO USE IT AND BECOME THE WORLD'S CHAMPION SKIPPER! EVEN BIGGER THAN THE ONE ON "GILLIGAN"!
IT'S THE JUMP ROPE THAT'S BIG, ORANGE! IT'S MUCH TOO BIG FOR YOU!
MK
IT IS?
OF COURSE IT IS! YOU'LL NEVER BE ABLE TO SKIP IT! TAKE IT BACK AND GO FIND SOME-THING MORE YOUR OWN SIZE!
IF YOU SAY SO, MR. SMARTY-PANTS.
SIGH...

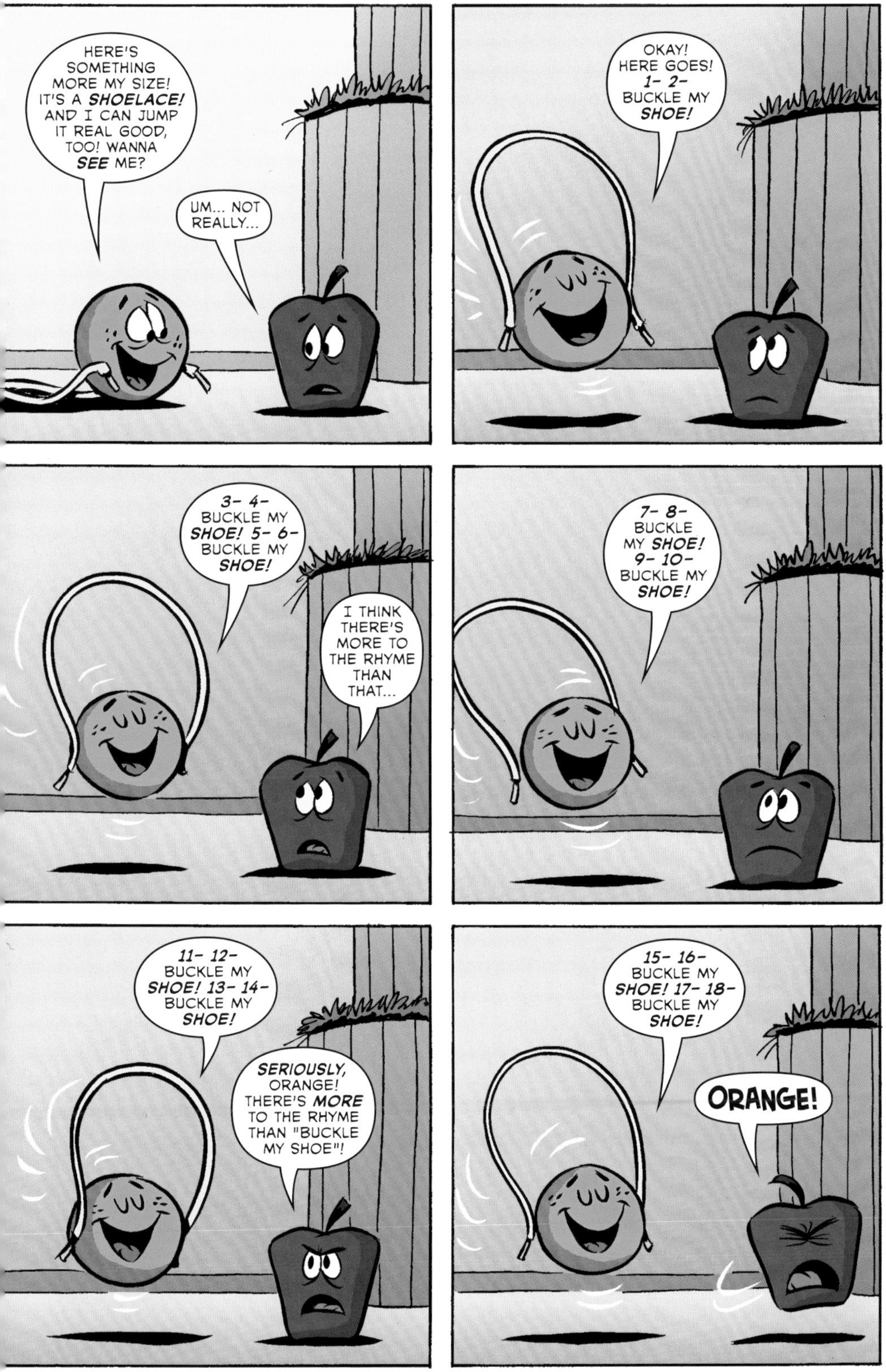
HERE'S SOMETHING MORE MY SIZE! IT'S A SHOELACE! AND I CAN JUMP IT REAL GOOD, TOO! WANNA SEE ME?
UM... NOT REALLY...
OKAY! HERE GOES! 1- 2- BUCKLE MY SHOE!
3- 4- BUCKLE MY SHOE! 5- 6- BUCKLE MY SHOE!
I THINK THERE'S MORE TO THE RHYME THAN THAT...
7- 8- BUCKLE MY SHOE! 9- 10- BUCKLE MY SHOE!
11- 12- BUCKLE MY SHOE! 13- 14- BUCKLE MY SHOE!
SERIOUSLY, ORANGE! THERE'S MORE TO THE RHYME THAN "BUCKLE MY SHOE"!
15- 16- BUCKLE MY SHOE! 17- 18- BUCKLE MY SHOE!
ORANGE!

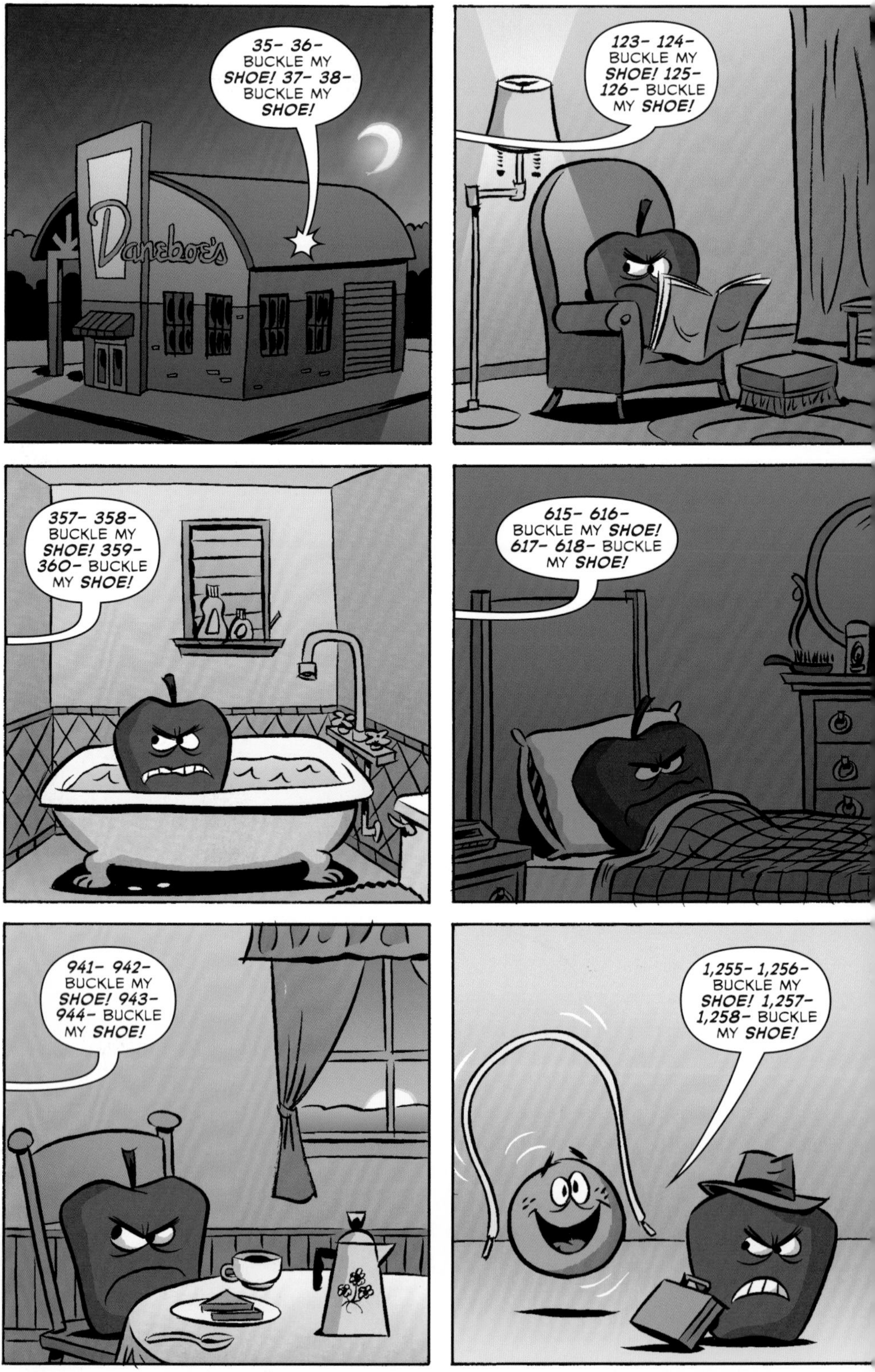
Danebore's
35- 36- BUCKLE MY SHOE! 37- 38- BUCKLE MY SHOE!
123- 124- BUCKLE MY SHOE! 125- 126- BUCKLE MY SHOE!
357- 358- BUCKLE MY SHOE! 359- 360- BUCKLE MY SHOE!
615- 616- BUCKLE MY SHOE! 617- 618- BUCKLE MY SHOE!
941- 942- BUCKLE MY SHOE! 943- 944- BUCKLE MY SHOE!
1,255- 1,256- BUCKLE MY SHOE! 1,257- 1,258- BUCKLE MY SHOE!

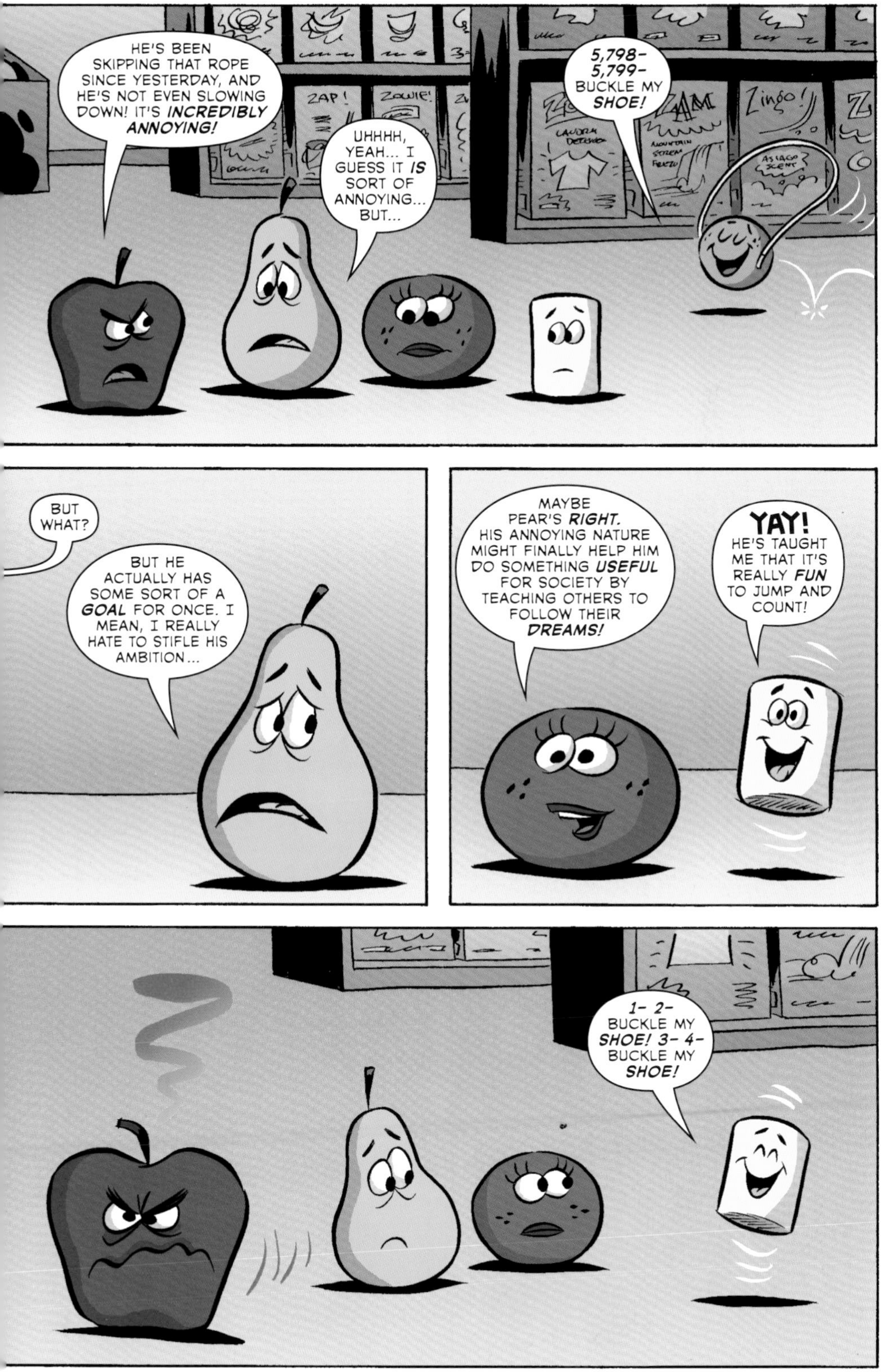

HE'S BEEN SKIPPING THAT ROPE SINCE YESTERDAY, AND HE'S NOT EVEN SLOWING DOWN! IT'S *INCREDIBLY ANNOYING!*
UHHHH, YEAH... I GUESS IT *IS* SORT OF ANNOYING... BUT...
5,798- 5,799- BUCKLE MY *SHOE!*
ZAP!
ZOWIE!
Zingo!
BUT WHAT?
BUT HE ACTUALLY HAS SOME SORT OF A *GOAL* FOR ONCE. I MEAN, I REALLY HATE TO STIFLE HIS AMBITION...
MAYBE PEAR'S *RIGHT.* HIS ANNOYING NATURE MIGHT FINALLY HELP HIM DO SOMETHING *USEFUL* FOR SOCIETY BY TEACHING OTHERS TO FOLLOW THEIR *DREAMS!*
YAY! HE'S TAUGHT ME THAT IT'S REALLY *FUN* TO JUMP AND COUNT!
1- 2- BUCKLE MY *SHOE!* 3- 4- BUCKLE MY *SHOE!*

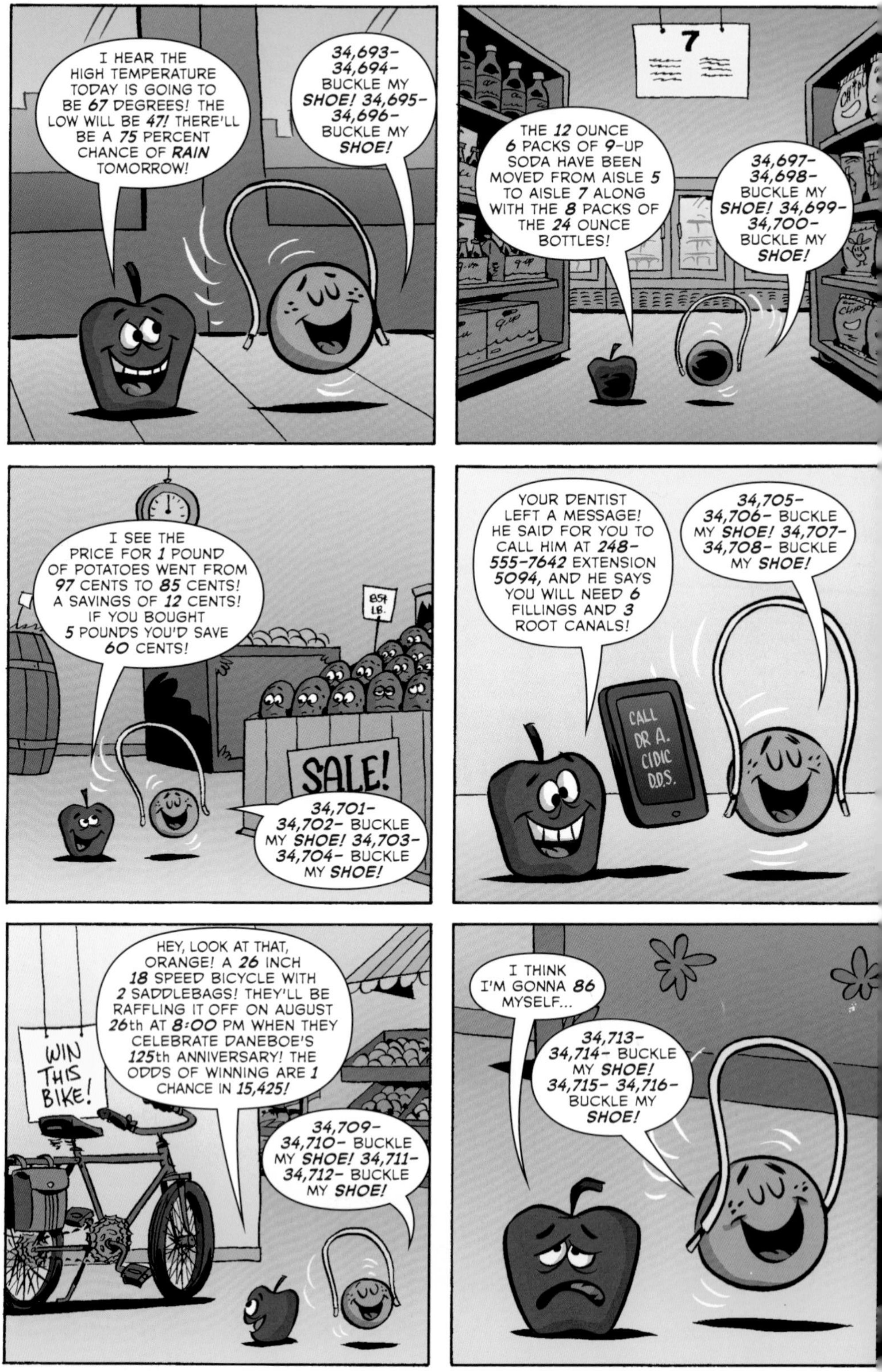
I HEAR THE HIGH TEMPERATURE TODAY IS GOING TO BE 67 DEGREES! THE LOW WILL BE 47! THERE'LL BE A 75 PERCENT CHANCE OF RAIN TOMORROW!
34,693- 34,694- BUCKLE MY SHOE! 34,695- 34,696- BUCKLE MY SHOE!
7
THE 12 OUNCE 6 PACKS OF 9-UP SODA HAVE BEEN MOVED FROM AISLE 5 TO AISLE 7 ALONG WITH THE 8 PACKS OF THE 24 OUNCE BOTTLES!
34,697- 34,698- BUCKLE MY SHOE! 34,699- 34,700- BUCKLE MY SHOE!
I SEE THE PRICE FOR 1 POUND OF POTATOES WENT FROM 97 CENTS TO 85 CENTS! A SAVINGS OF 12 CENTS! IF YOU BOUGHT 5 POUNDS YOU'D SAVE 60 CENTS!
SALE!
34,701- 34,702- BUCKLE MY SHOE! 34,703- 34,704- BUCKLE MY SHOE!
YOUR DENTIST LEFT A MESSAGE! HE SAID FOR YOU TO CALL HIM AT 248-555-7642 EXTENSION 5094, AND HE SAYS YOU WILL NEED 6 FILLINGS AND 3 ROOT CANALS!
34,705- 34,706- BUCKLE MY SHOE! 34,707- 34,708- BUCKLE MY SHOE!
CALL DR A. CIDIC D.D.S.
WIN THIS BIKE!
HEY, LOOK AT THAT, ORANGE! A 26 INCH 18 SPEED BICYCLE WITH 2 SADDLEBAGS! THEY'LL BE RAFFLING IT OFF ON AUGUST 26th AT 8:00 PM WHEN THEY CELEBRATE DANEBOE'S 125th ANNIVERSARY! THE ODDS OF WINNING ARE 1 CHANCE IN 15,425!
34,709- 34,710- BUCKLE MY SHOE! 34,711- 34,712- BUCKLE MY SHOE!
I THINK I'M GONNA 86 MYSELF...
34,713- 34,714- BUCKLE MY SHOE! 34,715- 34,716- BUCKLE MY SHOE!

34,712, er, no, it's just 12

SO HERE'S THE DEAL... I'LL PAY YOU **50 BUCKS** IF YOU'LL BEAT UP ORANGE AND TAKE AWAY HIS ***JUMP ROPE!***
NO WAY, MAN! I'M NOT ANYBODY'S ERRAND BOY! FIND YOURSELF ***ANOTHER*** FRUIT!
BUT... BUT I THOUGHT YOU ***HATED*** THAT GUY!
HEY THAT'S RIGHT! ***I DO!***
I'LL MAKE THAT SISSY CITRUS STOP ***COUNTING*** AND CRY ***"UNCLE"*** INSTEAD! JUST WATCH!
1,654,825- 1,654,826- BUCKLE MY ***SHOE!***
HEY ORANGE! I, GRAPEFRUIT, AM GONNA TAKE THAT STUPID ROPE ***AWAY*** FROM YOU AND THEN I'M GONNA STUFF IT DOWN YOUR--
1,654,827- 1,654,828- BUCKLE MY ***SHOE!***
THWACK
1,654,829- 1,654,830- BUCKLE MY ***SHOE!***
BAWW! THAT ***HURT!*** YOU DIDN'T SAY HE WAS GONNA ***FIGHT BACK!***

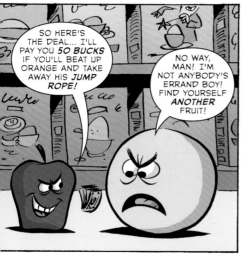

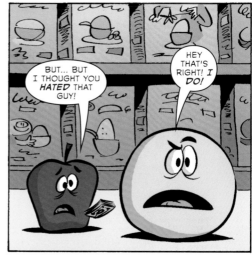

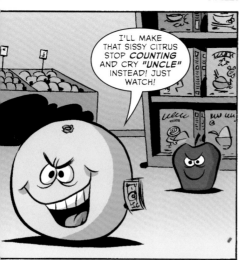

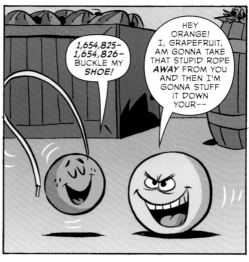

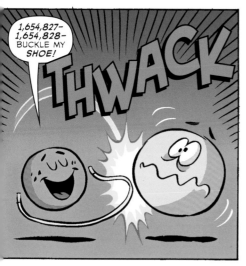

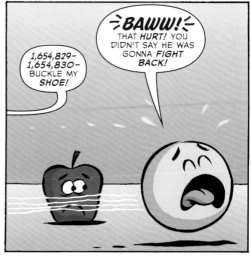

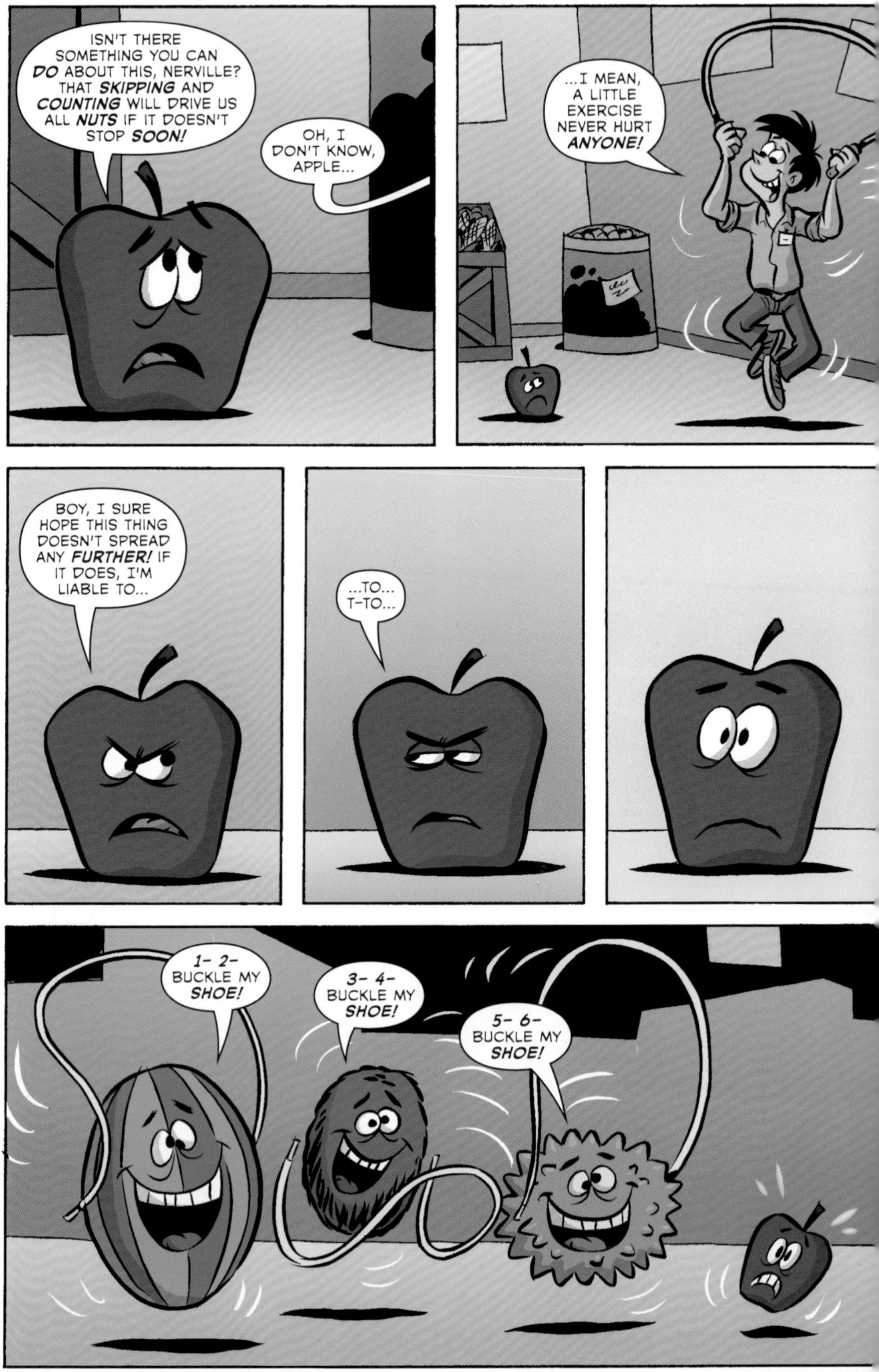
ISN'T THERE SOMETHING YOU CAN DO ABOUT THIS, NERVILLE? THAT SKIPPING AND COUNTING WILL DRIVE US ALL NUTS IF IT DOESN'T STOP SOON!
OH, I DON'T KNOW, APPLE...
...I MEAN, A LITTLE EXERCISE NEVER HURT ANYONE!
BOY, I SURE HOPE THIS THING DOESN'T SPREAD ANY FURTHER! IF IT DOES, I'M LIABLE TO...
...TO... T-TO...
1- 2- BUCKLE MY SHOE!
3- 4- BUCKLE MY SHOE!
5- 6- BUCKLE MY SHOE!

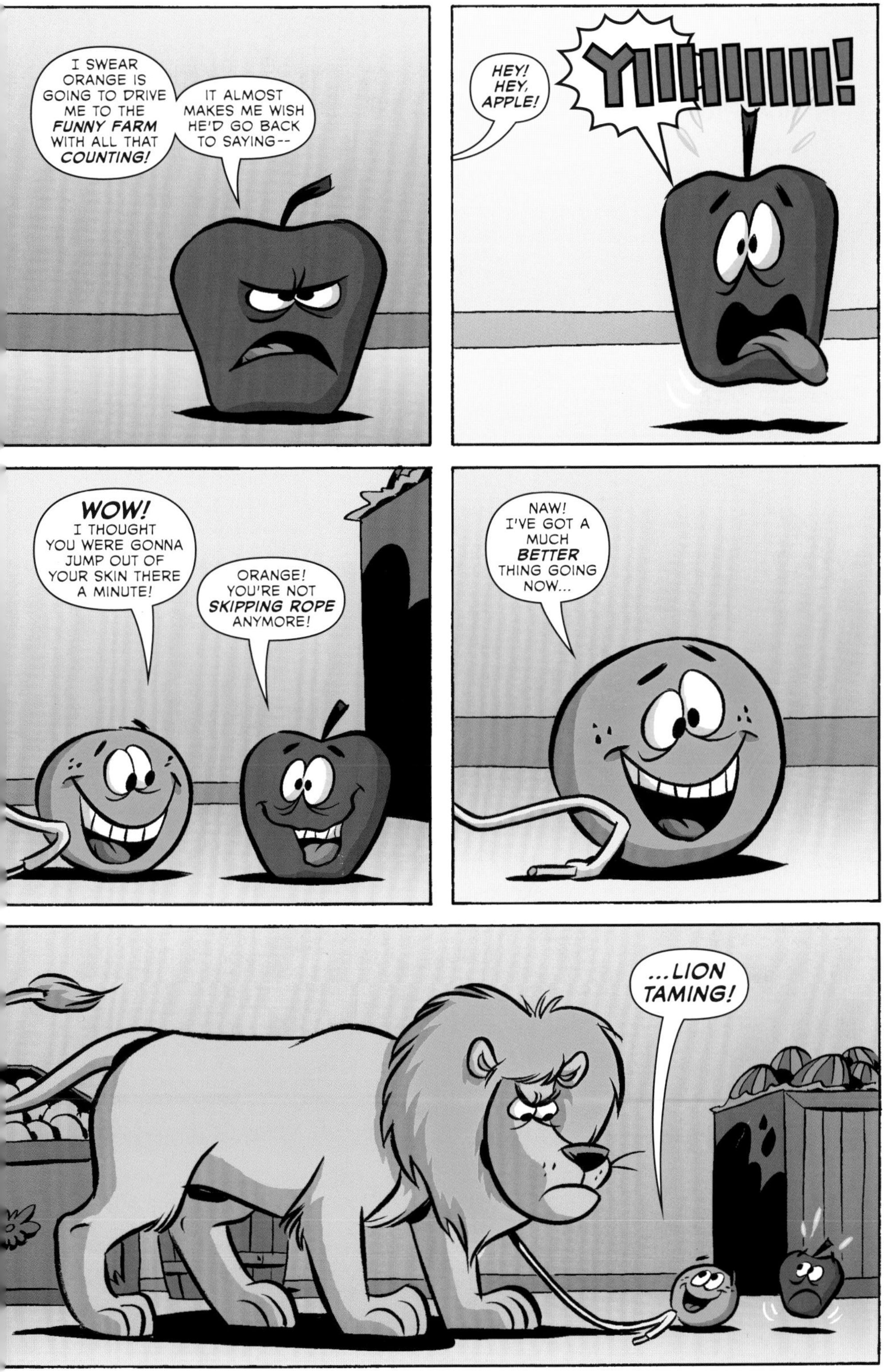
I SWEAR ORANGE IS GOING TO DRIVE ME TO THE FUNNY FARM WITH ALL THAT COUNTING!
IT ALMOST MAKES ME WISH HE'D GO BACK TO SAYING--
HEY! HEY, APPLE!
YIIIIIIIII!
WOW! I THOUGHT YOU WERE GONNA JUMP OUT OF YOUR SKIN THERE A MINUTE!
ORANGE! YOU'RE NOT SKIPPING ROPE ANYMORE!
NAW! I'VE GOT A MUCH BETTER THING GOING NOW...
...LION TAMING!

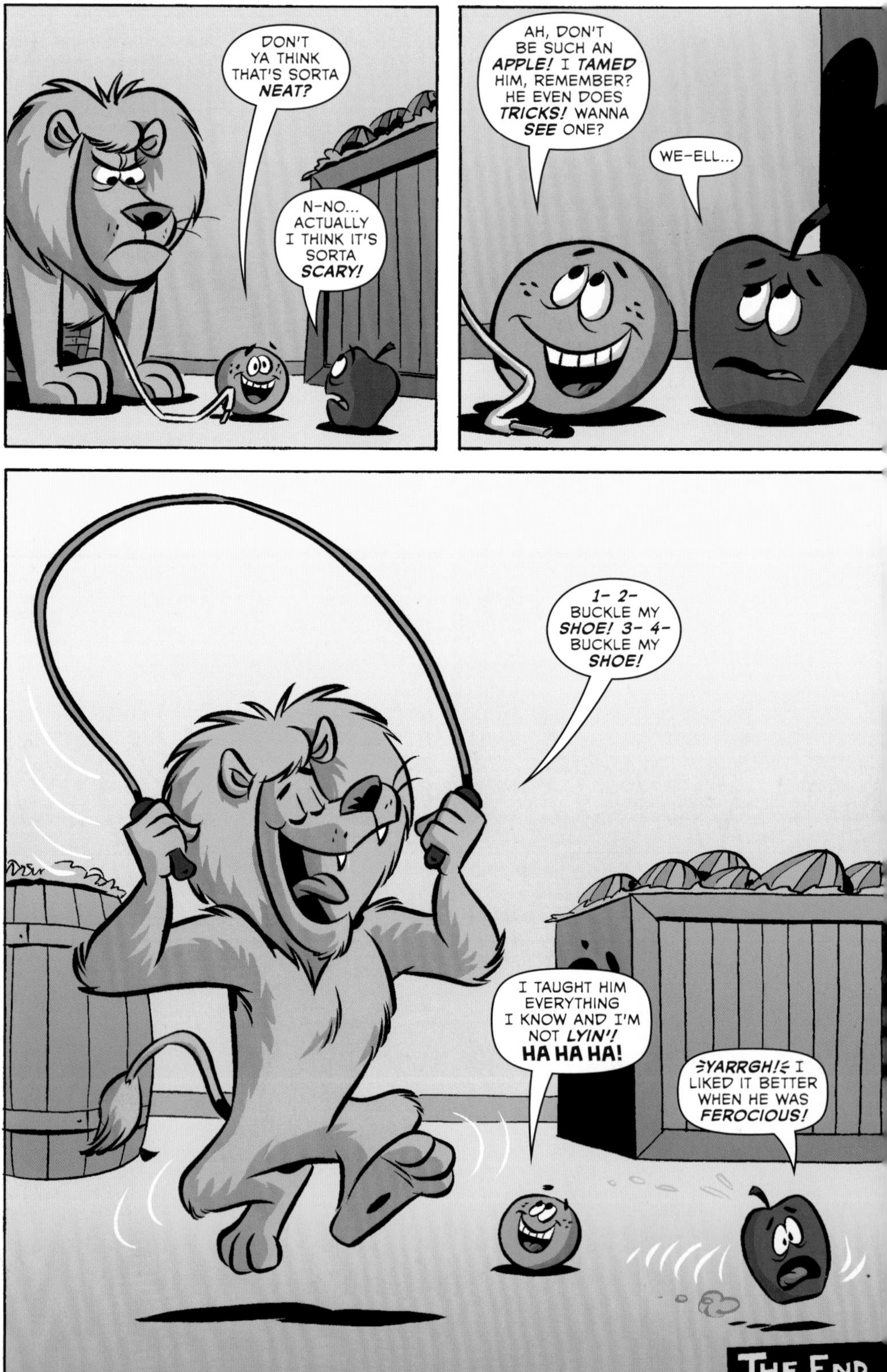
DON'T YA THINK THAT'S SORTA **NEAT?**
N-NO... ACTUALLY I THINK IT'S SORTA **SCARY!**
AH, DON'T BE SUCH AN **APPLE!** I **TAMED** HIM, REMEMBER? HE EVEN DOES **TRICKS!** WANNA **SEE** ONE?
WE-ELL...
1- 2- BUCKLE MY **SHOE! 3- 4-** BUCKLE MY **SHOE!**
I TAUGHT HIM EVERYTHING I KNOW AND I'M NOT **LYIN'!** **HA HA HA!**
YARRGH! I LIKED IT BETTER WHEN HE WAS **FEROCIOUS!**
THE END.

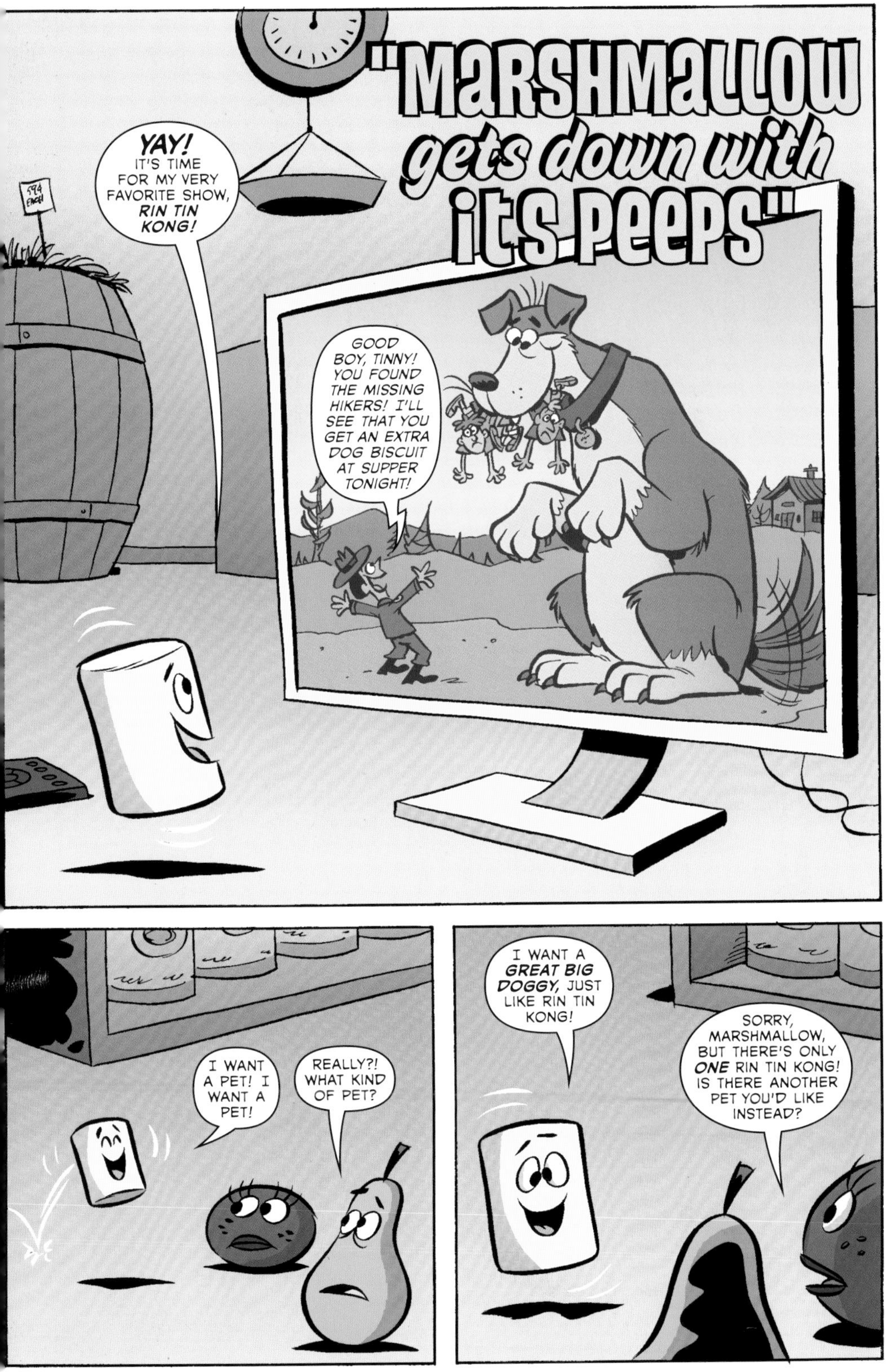

"MARSHMALLOW gets down with its PEEPS"
YAY! IT'S TIME FOR MY VERY FAVORITE SHOW, RIN TIN KONG!
GOOD BOY, TINNY! YOU FOUND THE MISSING HIKERS! I'LL SEE THAT YOU GET AN EXTRA DOG BISCUIT AT SUPPER TONIGHT!
I WANT A PET! I WANT A PET!
REALLY?! WHAT KIND OF PET?
I WANT A GREAT BIG DOGGY, JUST LIKE RIN TIN KONG!
SORRY, MARSHMALLOW, BUT THERE'S ONLY ONE RIN TIN KONG! IS THERE ANOTHER PET YOU'D LIKE INSTEAD?

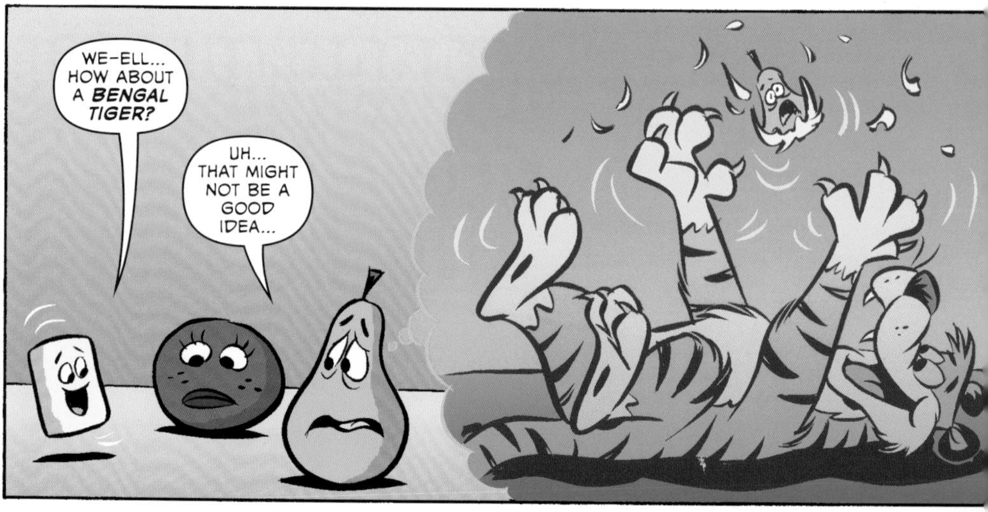
WE-ELL... HOW ABOUT A **BENGAL TIGER?**
UH... THAT MIGHT NOT BE A GOOD IDEA...

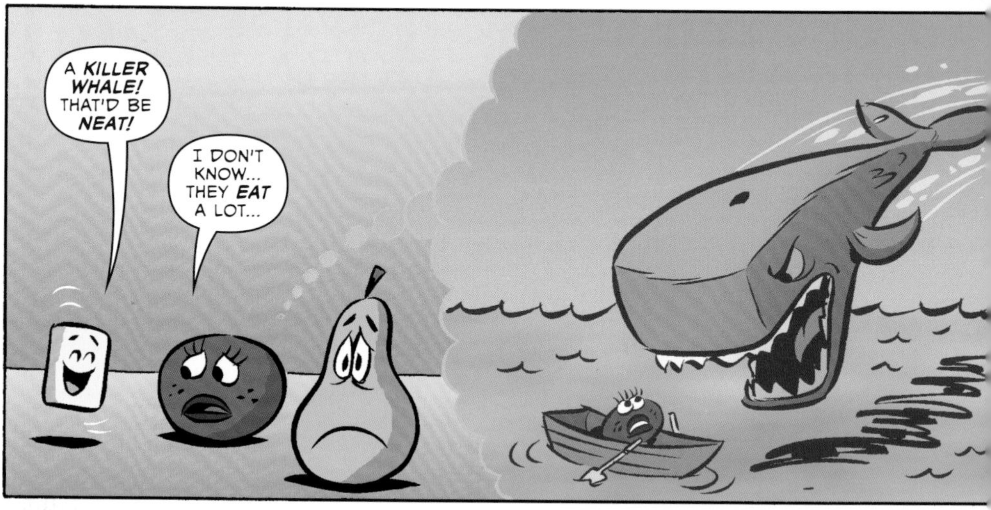
A **KILLER WHALE!** THAT'D BE **NEAT!**
I DON'T KNOW... THEY **EAT** A LOT...

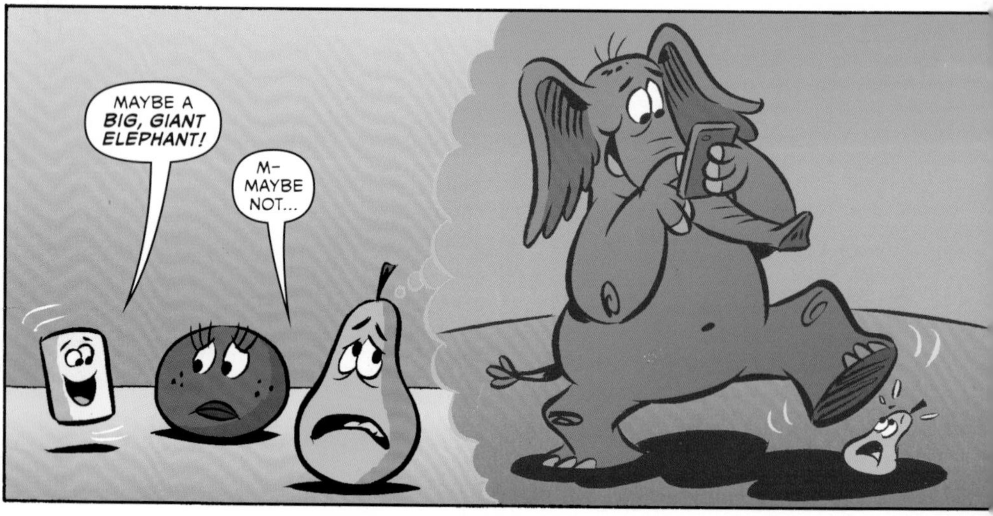
MAYBE A **BIG, GIANT ELEPHANT!**
M-MAYBE NOT...

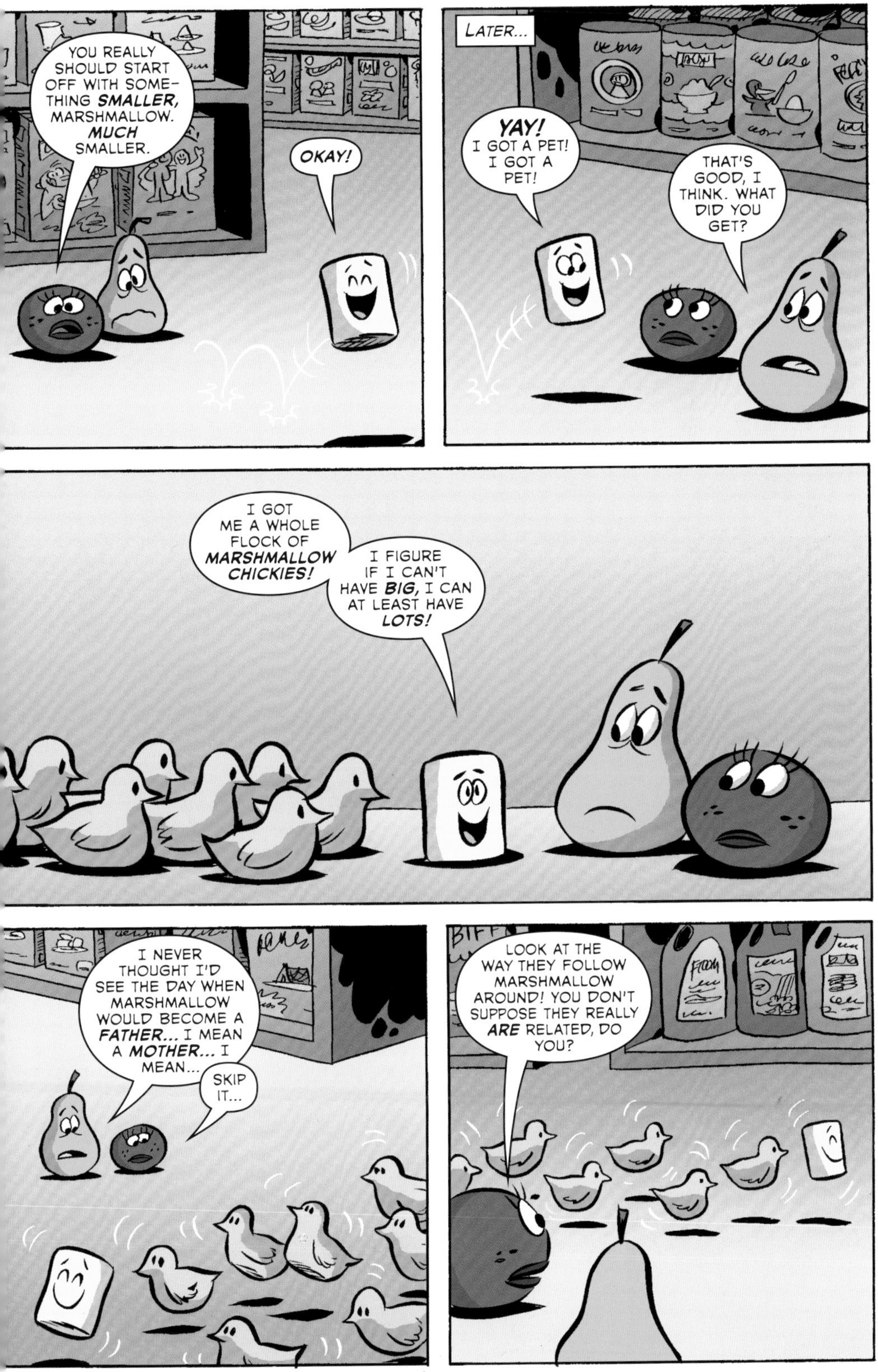
YOU REALLY SHOULD START OFF WITH SOMETHING SMALLER, MARSHMALLOW. MUCH SMALLER.
OKAY!
LATER...
YAY! I GOT A PET! I GOT A PET!
THAT'S GOOD, I THINK. WHAT DID YOU GET?
I GOT ME A WHOLE FLOCK OF MARSHMALLOW CHICKIES!
I FIGURE IF I CAN'T HAVE BIG, I CAN AT LEAST HAVE LOTS!
I NEVER THOUGHT I'D SEE THE DAY WHEN MARSHMALLOW WOULD BECOME A FATHER... I MEAN A MOTHER... I MEAN...
SKIP IT...
LOOK AT THE WAY THEY FOLLOW MARSHMALLOW AROUND! YOU DON'T SUPPOSE THEY REALLY ARE RELATED, DO YOU?

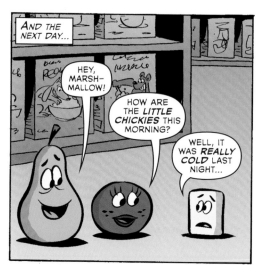

AND THE NEXT DAY...

HEY, MARSH-MALLOW!

HOW ARE THE *LITTLE CHICKIES* THIS MORNING?

WELL, IT WAS *REALLY COLD* LAST NIGHT...

SO I THOUGHT I'D KEEP MY LITTLE CHICKIES *WARM...*

...BY PUTTING THEM IN THE *MICRO-WAVE...*

MARSH-MALLOW! YOU *DIDN'T!*

AND GUESS WHAT? NOW NOT ONLY DO I HAVE *LOTS,* I HAVE *BIG,* TOO!

YAY!

END.

EARLY ONE FINE DAY IN THE PRODUCE DEPARTMENT OF DANEBOE'S SUPERMARKET...

HEY, EVERYBODY--

--I'M FINALLY BACK FROM MY *VACATION!*

YAY! *NERVILLE'S* BACK!

DID ANYONE MISS ME?

"MISS YOU"? AS IN, "I'D THROW A BRICK AT YOU BUT, I MIGHT *MISS* YOU"? HAHAHAHAHAHAHA!

SO, WHERE HAVE YOU BEEN, YOU WALKIN' *MEATBAG?*

I WAS OFF *SURFING!* AT THE BEACH! Y'KNOW, ON A SURFBOARD!

"BOARD"? I'M PLENTY *BORED,* ALL RIGHT-- THANKS TO NERVILLE! HAHAHAHAHAHAHA!

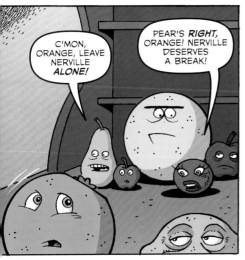

C'MON, ORANGE, LEAVE NERVILLE *ALONE!*

PEAR'S *RIGHT,* ORANGE! NERVILLE DESERVES A BREAK!

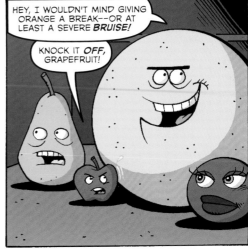

HEY, I WOULDN'T MIND GIVING ORANGE A BREAK--OR AT LEAST A SEVERE *BRUISE!*

KNOCK IT *OFF,* GRAPEFRUIT!

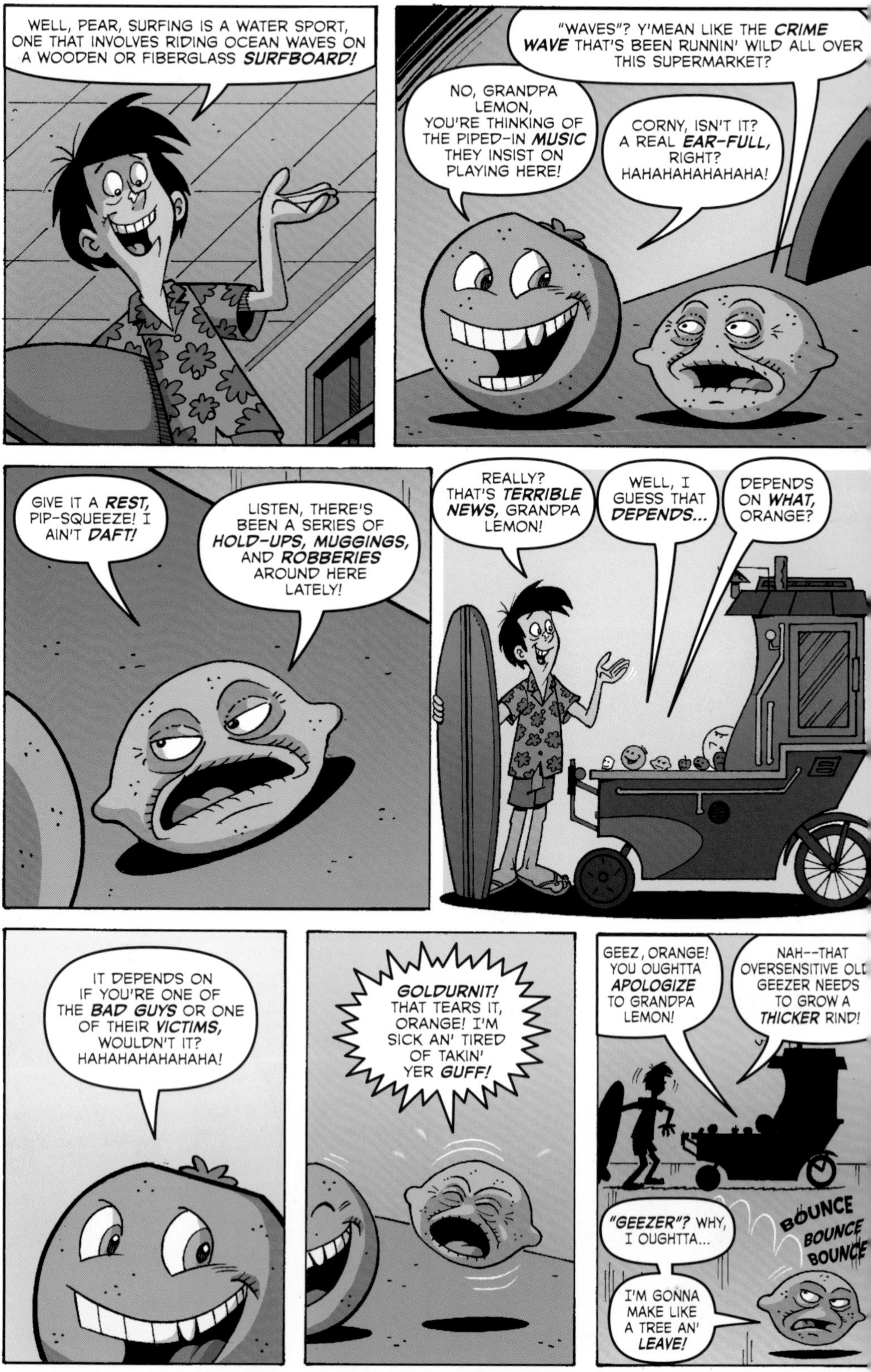
WELL, PEAR, SURFING IS A WATER SPORT, ONE THAT INVOLVES RIDING OCEAN WAVES ON A WOODEN OR FIBERGLASS SURFBOARD!
"WAVES"? Y'MEAN LIKE THE CRIME WAVE THAT'S BEEN RUNNIN' WILD ALL OVER THIS SUPERMARKET?
NO, GRANDPA LEMON, YOU'RE THINKING OF THE PIPED-IN MUSIC THEY INSIST ON PLAYING HERE!
CORNY, ISN'T IT? A REAL EAR-FULL, RIGHT? HAHAHAHAHAHAHA!
GIVE IT A REST, PIP-SQUEEZE! I AIN'T DAFT!
LISTEN, THERE'S BEEN A SERIES OF HOLD-UPS, MUGGINGS, AND ROBBERIES AROUND HERE LATELY!
REALLY? THAT'S TERRIBLE NEWS, GRANDPA LEMON!
WELL, I GUESS THAT DEPENDS...
DEPENDS ON WHAT, ORANGE?
IT DEPENDS ON IF YOU'RE ONE OF THE BAD GUYS OR ONE OF THEIR VICTIMS, WOULDN'T IT? HAHAHAHAHAHAHA!
GOLDURNIT! THAT TEARS IT, ORANGE! I'M SICK AN' TIRED OF TAKIN' YER GUFF!
GEEZ, ORANGE! YOU OUGHTTA APOLOGIZE TO GRANDPA LEMON!
NAH--THAT OVERSENSITIVE OLD GEEZER NEEDS TO GROW A THICKER RIND!
"GEEZER"? WHY, I OUGHTTA...
I'M GONNA MAKE LIKE A TREE AN' LEAVE!
BOUNCE BOUNCE BOUNCE

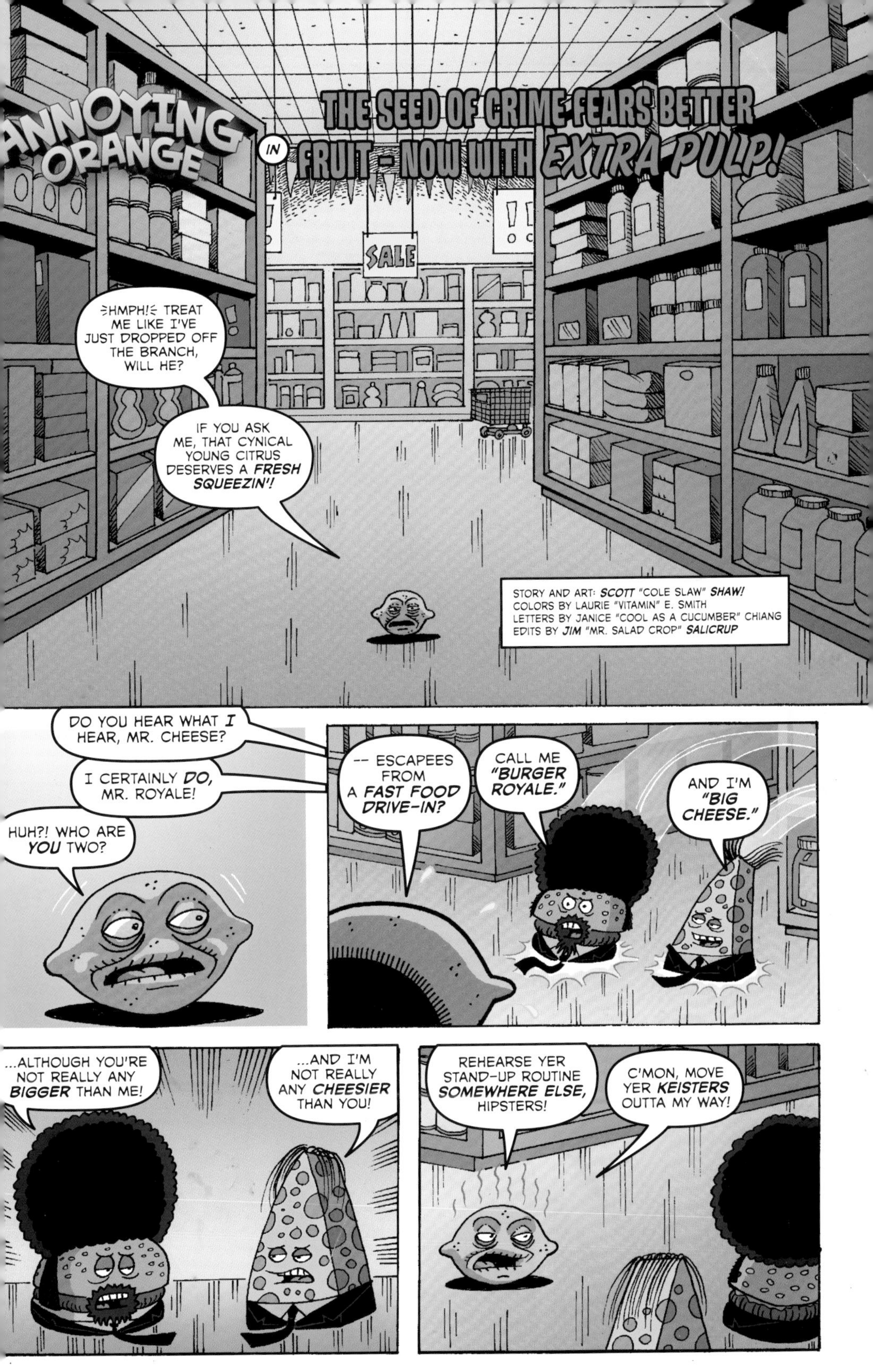
ANNOYING ORANGE
IN
THE SEED OF CRIME FEARS BETTER FRUIT - NOW WITH EXTRA PULP!
SALE
HMPH! TREAT ME LIKE I'VE JUST DROPPED OFF THE BRANCH, WILL HE?
IF YOU ASK ME, THAT CYNICAL YOUNG CITRUS DESERVES A FRESH SQUEEZIN'!
STORY AND ART: SCOTT "COLE SLAW" SHAW!
COLORS BY LAURIE "VITAMIN" E. SMITH
LETTERS BY JANICE "COOL AS A CUCUMBER" CHIANG
EDITS BY JIM "MR. SALAD CROP" SALICRUP
DO YOU HEAR WHAT I HEAR, MR. CHEESE?
I CERTAINLY DO, MR. ROYALE!
HUH?! WHO ARE YOU TWO?
-- ESCAPEES FROM A FAST FOOD DRIVE-IN?
CALL ME "BURGER ROYALE."
AND I'M "BIG CHEESE."
...ALTHOUGH YOU'RE NOT REALLY ANY BIGGER THAN ME!
...AND I'M NOT REALLY ANY CHEESIER THAN YOU!
REHEARSE YER STAND-UP ROUTINE SOMEWHERE ELSE, HIPSTERS!
C'MON, MOVE YER KEISTERS OUTTA MY WAY!

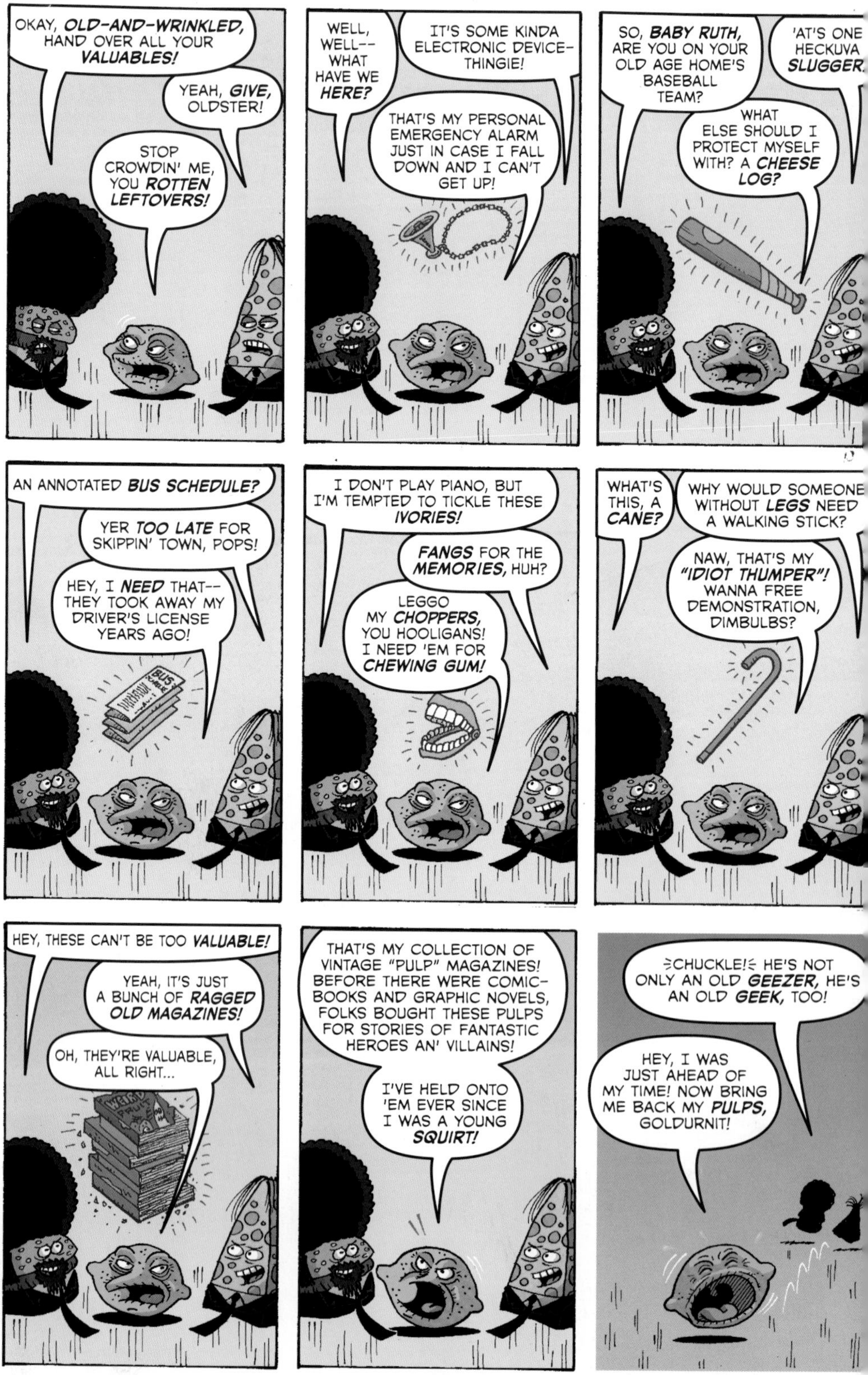
OKAY, OLD-AND-WRINKLED, HAND OVER ALL YOUR VALUABLES!
YEAH, GIVE, OLDSTER!
STOP CROWDIN' ME, YOU ROTTEN LEFTOVERS!
WELL, WELL-- WHAT HAVE WE HERE?
IT'S SOME KINDA ELECTRONIC DEVICE-THINGIE!
THAT'S MY PERSONAL EMERGENCY ALARM JUST IN CASE I FALL DOWN AND I CAN'T GET UP!
SO, BABY RUTH, ARE YOU ON YOUR OLD AGE HOME'S BASEBALL TEAM?
'AT'S ONE HECKUVA SLUGGER.
WHAT ELSE SHOULD I PROTECT MYSELF WITH? A CHEESE LOG?
AN ANNOTATED BUS SCHEDULE?
YER TOO LATE FOR SKIPPIN' TOWN, POPS!
HEY, I NEED THAT-- THEY TOOK AWAY MY DRIVER'S LICENSE YEARS AGO!
I DON'T PLAY PIANO, BUT I'M TEMPTED TO TICKLE THESE IVORIES!
FANGS FOR THE MEMORIES, HUH?
LEGGO MY CHOPPERS, YOU HOOLIGANS! I NEED 'EM FOR CHEWING GUM!
WHAT'S THIS, A CANE?
WHY WOULD SOMEONE WITHOUT LEGS NEED A WALKING STICK?
NAW, THAT'S MY "IDIOT THUMPER"! WANNA FREE DEMONSTRATION, DIMBULBS?
HEY, THESE CAN'T BE TOO VALUABLE!
YEAH, IT'S JUST A BUNCH OF RAGGED OLD MAGAZINES!
OH, THEY'RE VALUABLE, ALL RIGHT...
THAT'S MY COLLECTION OF VINTAGE "PULP" MAGAZINES! BEFORE THERE WERE COMIC-BOOKS AND GRAPHIC NOVELS, FOLKS BOUGHT THESE PULPS FOR STORIES OF FANTASTIC HEROES AN' VILLAINS!
I'VE HELD ONTO 'EM EVER SINCE I WAS A YOUNG SQUIRT!
CHUCKLE! HE'S NOT ONLY AN OLD GEEZER, HE'S AN OLD GEEK, TOO!
HEY, I WAS JUST AHEAD OF MY TIME! NOW BRING ME BACK MY PULPS, GOLDURNIT!

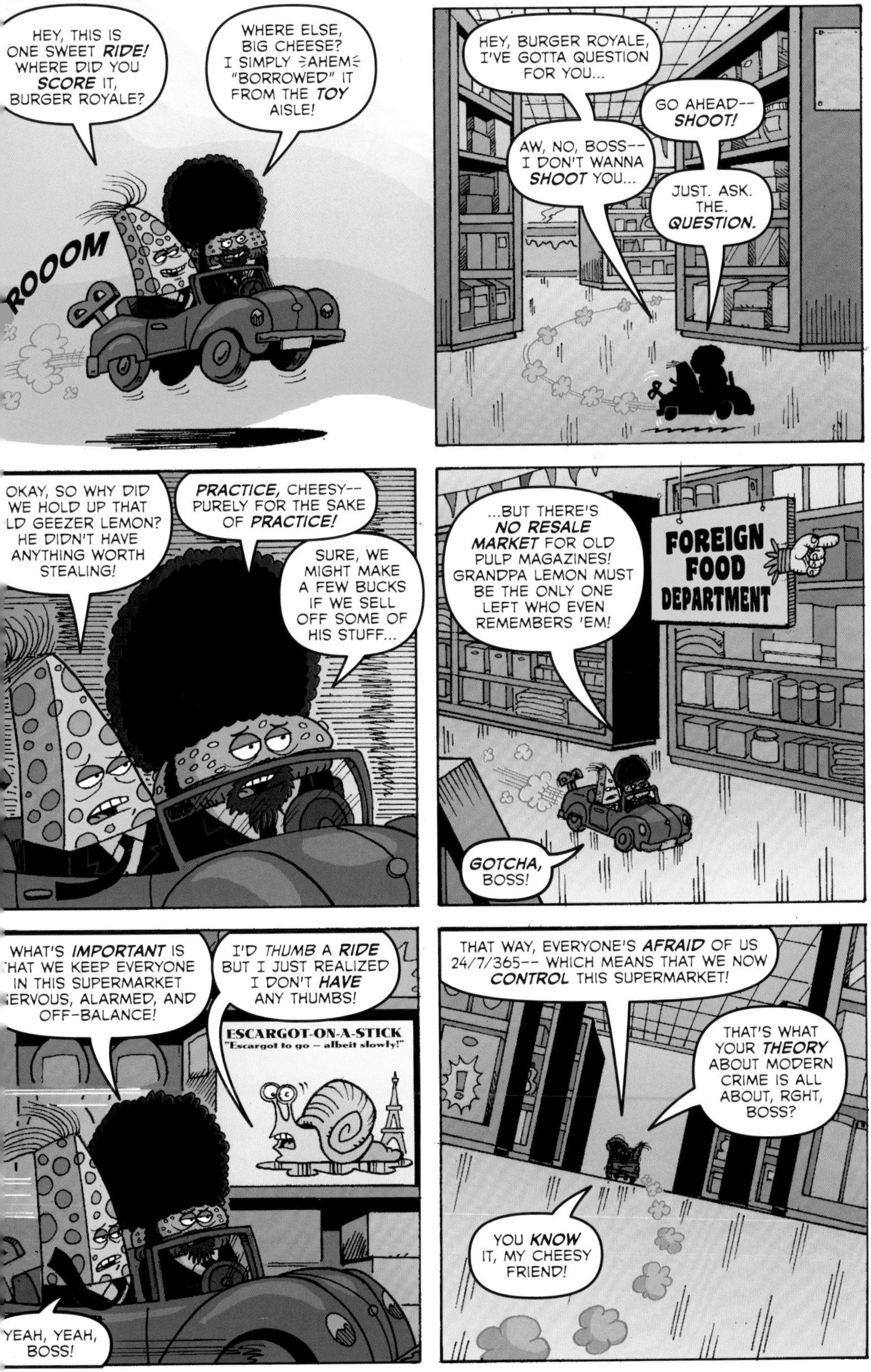
HEY, THIS IS ONE SWEET RIDE! WHERE DID YOU SCORE IT, BURGER ROYALE?
WHERE ELSE, BIG CHEESE? I SIMPLY AHEM "BORROWED" IT FROM THE TOY AISLE!
ROOOM
HEY, BURGER ROYALE, I'VE GOTTA QUESTION FOR YOU...
GO AHEAD-- SHOOT!
AW, NO, BOSS-- I DON'T WANNA SHOOT YOU...
JUST. ASK. THE. QUESTION.
OKAY, SO WHY DID WE HOLD UP THAT LD GEEZER LEMON? HE DIDN'T HAVE ANYTHING WORTH STEALING!
PRACTICE, CHEESY-- PURELY FOR THE SAKE OF PRACTICE!
SURE, WE MIGHT MAKE A FEW BUCKS IF WE SELL OFF SOME OF HIS STUFF...
...BUT THERE'S NO RESALE MARKET FOR OLD PULP MAGAZINES! GRANDPA LEMON MUST BE THE ONLY ONE LEFT WHO EVEN REMEMBERS 'EM!
FOREIGN FOOD DEPARTMENT
GOTCHA, BOSS!
WHAT'S IMPORTANT IS HAT WE KEEP EVERYONE IN THIS SUPERMARKET ERVOUS, ALARMED, AND OFF-BALANCE!
I'D THUMB A RIDE BUT I JUST REALIZED I DON'T HAVE ANY THUMBS!
ESCARGOT-ON-A-STICK
"Escargot to go — albeit slowly!"
YEAH, YEAH, BOSS!
THAT WAY, EVERYONE'S AFRAID OF US 24/7/365-- WHICH MEANS THAT WE NOW CONTROL THIS SUPERMARKET!
THAT'S WHAT YOUR THEORY ABOUT MODERN CRIME IS ALL ABOUT, RGHT, BOSS?
YOU KNOW IT, MY CHEESY FRIEND!

LATER... SO **THEN** I SAID TO HIM, "WHY, GRANDPA LEMON, I NEVER KNEW--"

THAT'S **RIGHT**, ORANGE--YOU NEVER **DO** KNOW!

G-GRANDPA L-L-LEMON?

DERN **RIGHT** IT'S ME, ORANGE.

HEY, IT'S G-GOOD TO SEE YOU, OLD-TIMER! YOU'RE LOOKING **YELLOW**, ER, **MELLOW**! HAHAHAHA!

Y'KNOW, I'M G-GLAD YOU'RE HERE BECAUSE I'VE BEEN MEANING TO **APOLOGIZE** TO YOU FOR THE WAY I--

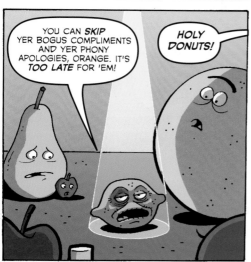

YOU CAN **SKIP** YER BOGUS COMPLIMENTS AND YER PHONY APOLOGIES, ORANGE. IT'S **TOO LATE** FOR 'EM!

HOLY DONUTS!

WHAT **HAPPENED** TO YOU, GRANDPA LEMON?!

I RAN INTO THAT TWO-MAN **CRIME WAVE** I WARNED YOU ABOUT. **THAT'S** WHAT HAPPENED, JUNIOR.

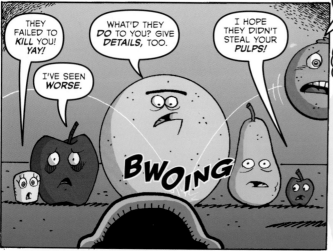

THEY FAILED TO **KILL** YOU! YAY!

I'VE SEEN **WORSE**.

WHAT'D THEY **DO** TO YOU? GIVE **DETAILS**, TOO.

I HOPE THEY DIDN'T STEAL YOUR **PULPS**!

BWOING

YEAH, WHAT **THEY** SAID, GRANDPA LEMON! **ALL** OF THEM!

SO MUCH FOR MAKING 'EM ALL FEEL **GUILTY**. THEY'RE NO HELP AT **ALL**! BUT I BET I KNOW WHO CAN HELP ME **STOP** THEM HIPSTER CROOKS FER GOOD!

26

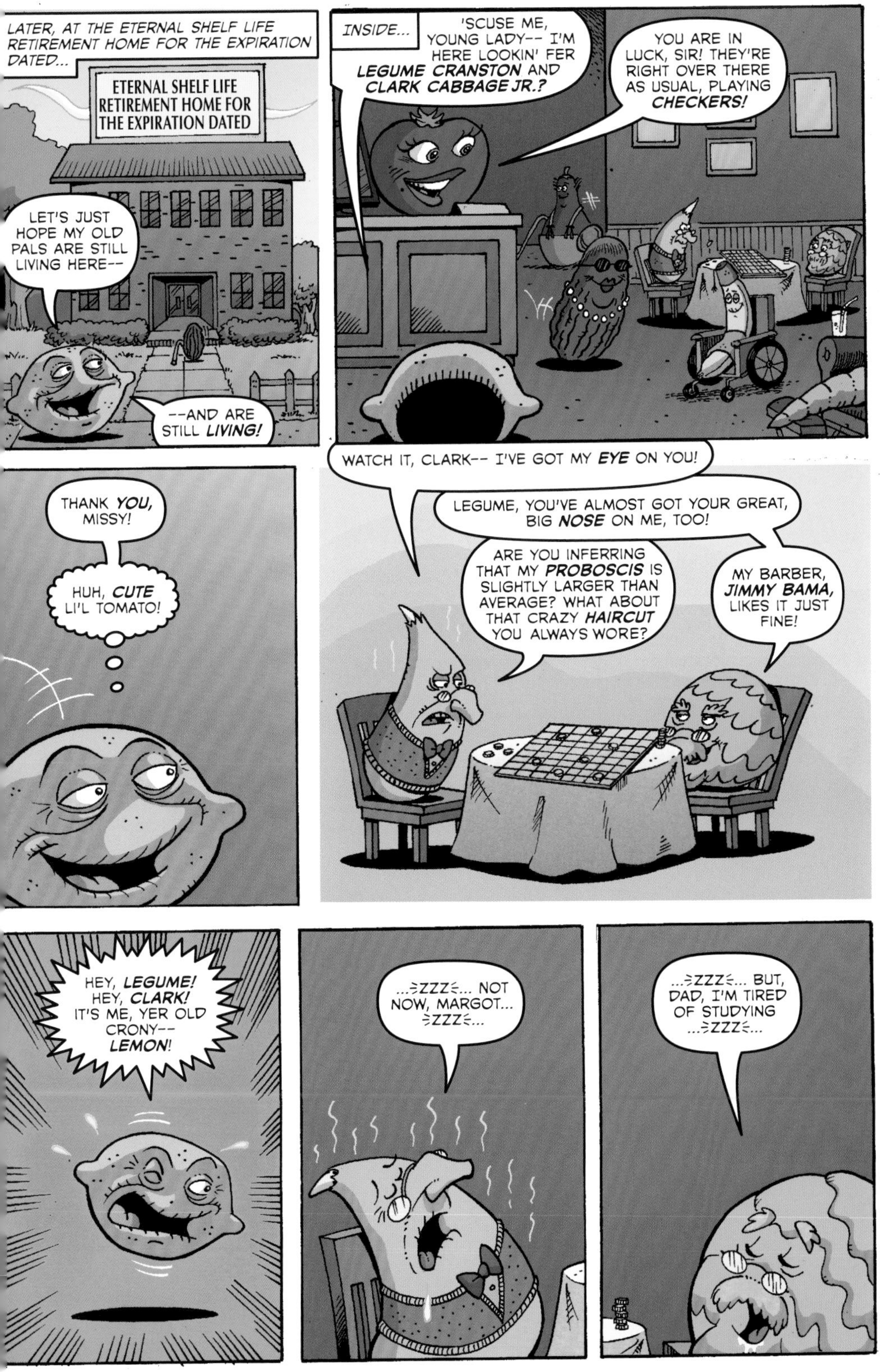
LATER, AT THE ETERNAL SHELF LIFE RETIREMENT HOME FOR THE EXPIRATION DATED...
ETERNAL SHELF LIFE RETIREMENT HOME FOR THE EXPIRATION DATED
LET'S JUST HOPE MY OLD PALS ARE STILL LIVING HERE--
--AND ARE STILL LIVING!
INSIDE...
'SCUSE ME, YOUNG LADY-- I'M HERE LOOKIN' FER LEGUME CRANSTON AND CLARK CABBAGE JR.?
YOU ARE IN LUCK, SIR! THEY'RE RIGHT OVER THERE AS USUAL, PLAYING CHECKERS!
THANK YOU, MISSY!
HUH, CUTE LI'L TOMATO!
WATCH IT, CLARK-- I'VE GOT MY EYE ON YOU!
LEGUME, YOU'VE ALMOST GOT YOUR GREAT, BIG NOSE ON ME, TOO!
ARE YOU INFERRING THAT MY PROBOSCIS IS SLIGHTLY LARGER THAN AVERAGE? WHAT ABOUT THAT CRAZY HAIRCUT YOU ALWAYS WORE?
MY BARBER, JIMMY BAMA, LIKES IT JUST FINE!
HEY, LEGUME! HEY, CLARK! IT'S ME, YER OLD CRONY-- LEMON!
...ZZZ... NOT NOW, MARGOT... ZZZ...
...ZZZ... BUT, DAD, I'M TIRED OF STUDYING ...ZZZ...

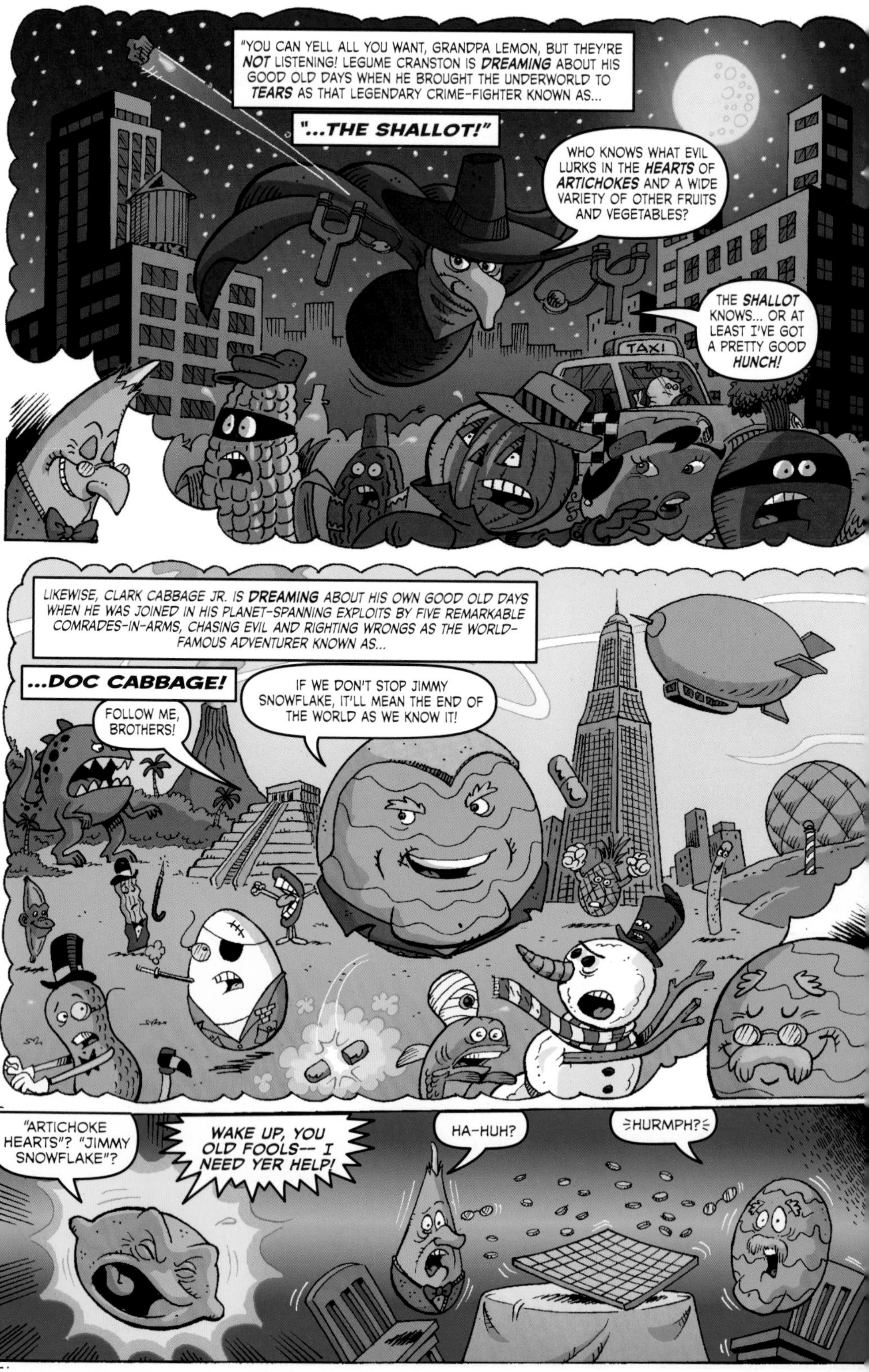
"YOU CAN YELL ALL YOU WANT, GRANDPA LEMON, BUT THEY'RE NOT LISTENING! LEGUME CRANSTON IS DREAMING ABOUT HIS GOOD OLD DAYS WHEN HE BROUGHT THE UNDERWORLD TO TEARS AS THAT LEGENDARY CRIME-FIGHTER KNOWN AS...
"...THE SHALLOT!"
WHO KNOWS WHAT EVIL LURKS IN THE HEARTS OF ARTICHOKES AND A WIDE VARIETY OF OTHER FRUITS AND VEGETABLES?
TAXI
THE SHALLOT KNOWS... OR AT LEAST I'VE GOT A PRETTY GOOD HUNCH!
LIKEWISE, CLARK CABBAGE JR. IS DREAMING ABOUT HIS OWN GOOD OLD DAYS WHEN HE WAS JOINED IN HIS PLANET-SPANNING EXPLOITS BY FIVE REMARKABLE COMRADES-IN-ARMS, CHASING EVIL AND RIGHTING WRONGS AS THE WORLD-FAMOUS ADVENTURER KNOWN AS...
...DOC CABBAGE!
FOLLOW ME, BROTHERS!
IF WE DON'T STOP JIMMY SNOWFLAKE, IT'LL MEAN THE END OF THE WORLD AS WE KNOW IT!
"ARTICHOKE HEARTS"? "JIMMY SNOWFLAKE"?
WAKE UP, YOU OLD FOOLS-- I NEED YER HELP!
HA-HUH?
HURMPH?

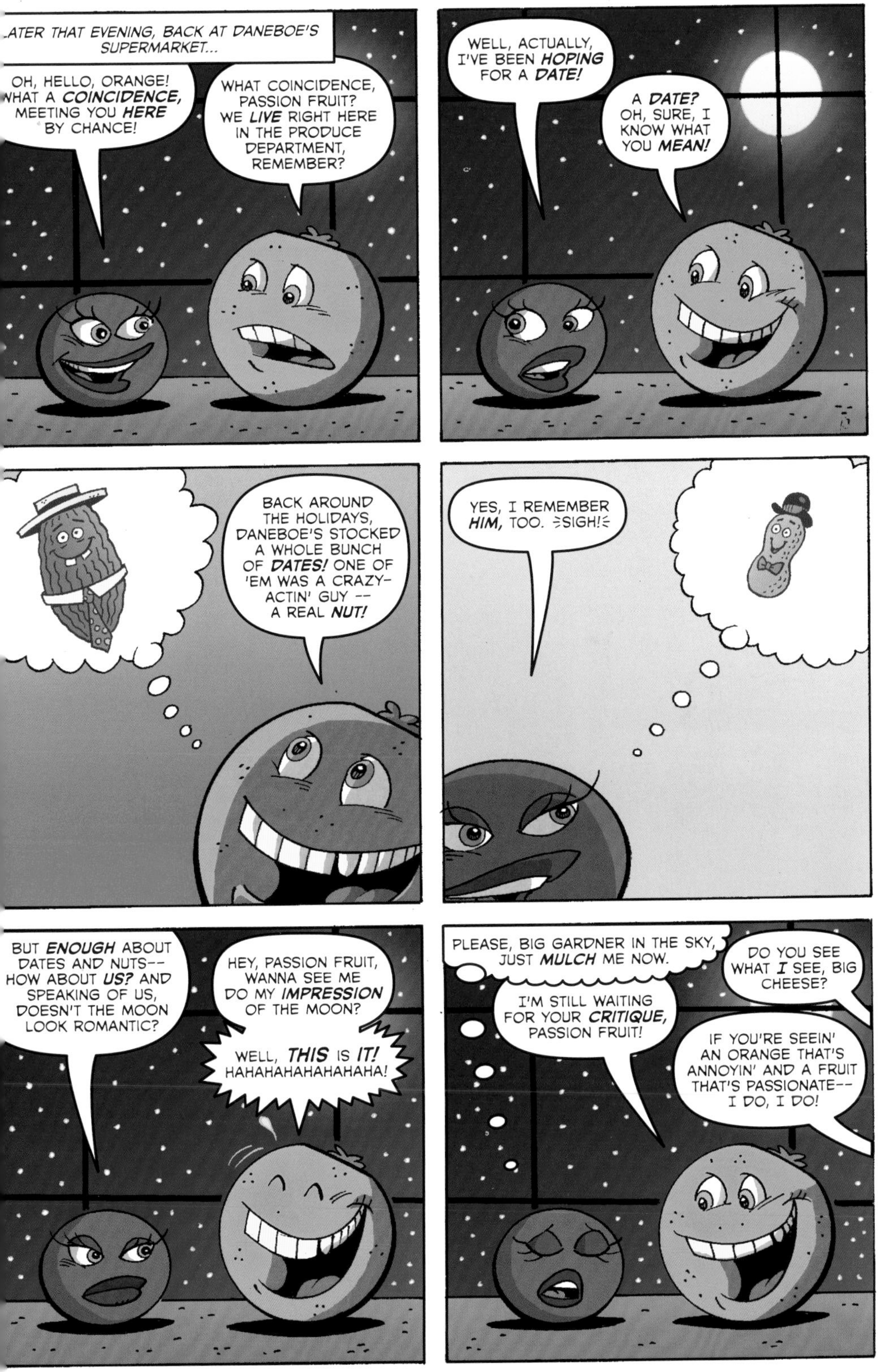

LATER THAT EVENING, BACK AT DANEBOE'S SUPERMARKET...
OH, HELLO, ORANGE! WHAT A COINCIDENCE, MEETING YOU HERE BY CHANCE!
WHAT COINCIDENCE, PASSION FRUIT? WE LIVE RIGHT HERE IN THE PRODUCE DEPARTMENT, REMEMBER?
WELL, ACTUALLY, I'VE BEEN HOPING FOR A DATE!
A DATE? OH, SURE, I KNOW WHAT YOU MEAN!
BACK AROUND THE HOLIDAYS, DANEBOE'S STOCKED A WHOLE BUNCH OF DATES! ONE OF 'EM WAS A CRAZY-ACTIN' GUY -- A REAL NUT!
YES, I REMEMBER HIM, TOO. SIGH!
BUT ENOUGH ABOUT DATES AND NUTS-- HOW ABOUT US? AND SPEAKING OF US, DOESN'T THE MOON LOOK ROMANTIC?
HEY, PASSION FRUIT, WANNA SEE ME DO MY IMPRESSION OF THE MOON?
WELL, THIS IS IT! HAHAHAHAHAHAHAHA!
PLEASE, BIG GARDNER IN THE SKY, JUST MULCH ME NOW.
I'M STILL WAITING FOR YOUR CRITIQUE, PASSION FRUIT!
DO YOU SEE WHAT I SEE, BIG CHEESE?
IF YOU'RE SEEIN' AN ORANGE THAT'S ANNOYIN' AND A FRUIT THAT'S PASSIONATE-- I DO, I DO!

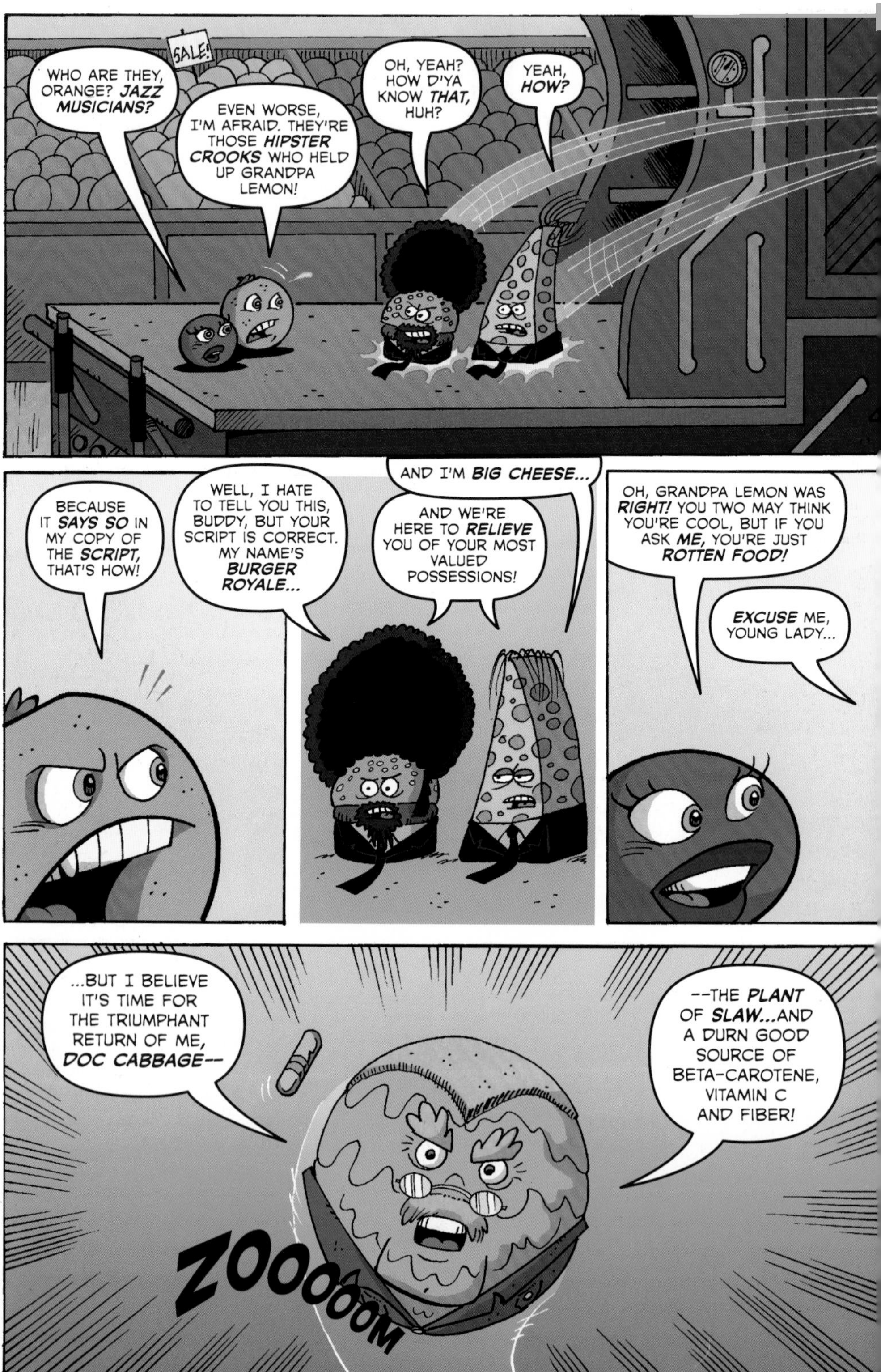
SALE!
WHO ARE THEY, ORANGE? JAZZ MUSICIANS?
EVEN WORSE, I'M AFRAID. THEY'RE THOSE HIPSTER CROOKS WHO HELD UP GRANDPA LEMON!
OH, YEAH? HOW D'YA KNOW THAT, HUH?
YEAH, HOW?
BECAUSE IT SAYS SO IN MY COPY OF THE SCRIPT, THAT'S HOW!
WELL, I HATE TO TELL YOU THIS, BUDDY, BUT YOUR SCRIPT IS CORRECT. MY NAME'S BURGER ROYALE...
AND I'M BIG CHEESE...
AND WE'RE HERE TO RELIEVE YOU OF YOUR MOST VALUED POSSESSIONS!
OH, GRANDPA LEMON WAS RIGHT! YOU TWO MAY THINK YOU'RE COOL, BUT IF YOU ASK ME, YOU'RE JUST ROTTEN FOOD!
EXCUSE ME, YOUNG LADY...
...BUT I BELIEVE IT'S TIME FOR THE TRIUMPHANT RETURN OF ME, DOC CABBAGE--
--THE PLANT OF SLAW...AND A DURN GOOD SOURCE OF BETA-CAROTENE, VITAMIN C AND FIBER!
ZOOOOOOM

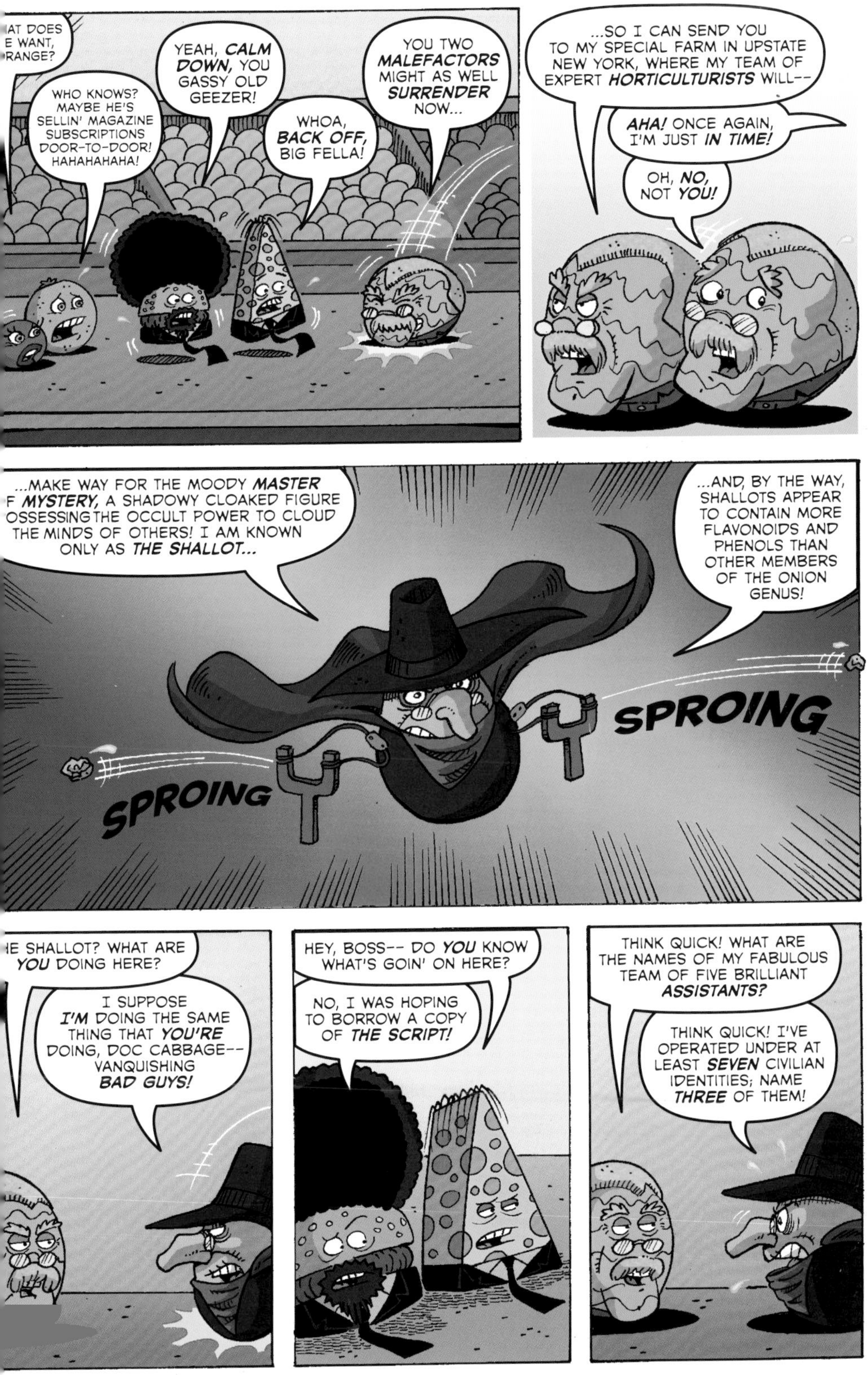

AT DOES
E WANT,
RANGE?
WHO KNOWS? MAYBE HE'S SELLIN' MAGAZINE SUBSCRIPTIONS DOOR-TO-DOOR! HAHAHAHAHA!
YEAH, CALM DOWN, YOU GASSY OLD GEEZER!
WHOA, BACK OFF, BIG FELLA!
YOU TWO MALEFACTORS MIGHT AS WELL SURRENDER NOW...
...SO I CAN SEND YOU TO MY SPECIAL FARM IN UPSTATE NEW YORK, WHERE MY TEAM OF EXPERT HORTICULTURISTS WILL--
AHA! ONCE AGAIN, I'M JUST IN TIME!
OH, NO, NOT YOU!
...MAKE WAY FOR THE MOODY MASTER
F MYSTERY, A SHADOWY CLOAKED FIGURE
OSSESSING THE OCCULT POWER TO CLOUD THE MINDS OF OTHERS! I AM KNOWN ONLY AS THE SHALLOT...
...AND, BY THE WAY, SHALLOTS APPEAR TO CONTAIN MORE FLAVONOIDS AND PHENOLS THAN OTHER MEMBERS OF THE ONION GENUS!
SPROING
SPROING
IE SHALLOT? WHAT ARE YOU DOING HERE?
I SUPPOSE I'M DOING THE SAME THING THAT YOU'RE DOING, DOC CABBAGE-- VANQUISHING BAD GUYS!
HEY, BOSS-- DO YOU KNOW WHAT'S GOIN' ON HERE?
NO, I WAS HOPING TO BORROW A COPY OF THE SCRIPT!
THINK QUICK! WHAT ARE THE NAMES OF MY FABULOUS TEAM OF FIVE BRILLIANT ASSISTANTS?
THINK QUICK! I'VE OPERATED UNDER AT LEAST SEVEN CIVILIAN IDENTITIES; NAME THREE OF THEM!

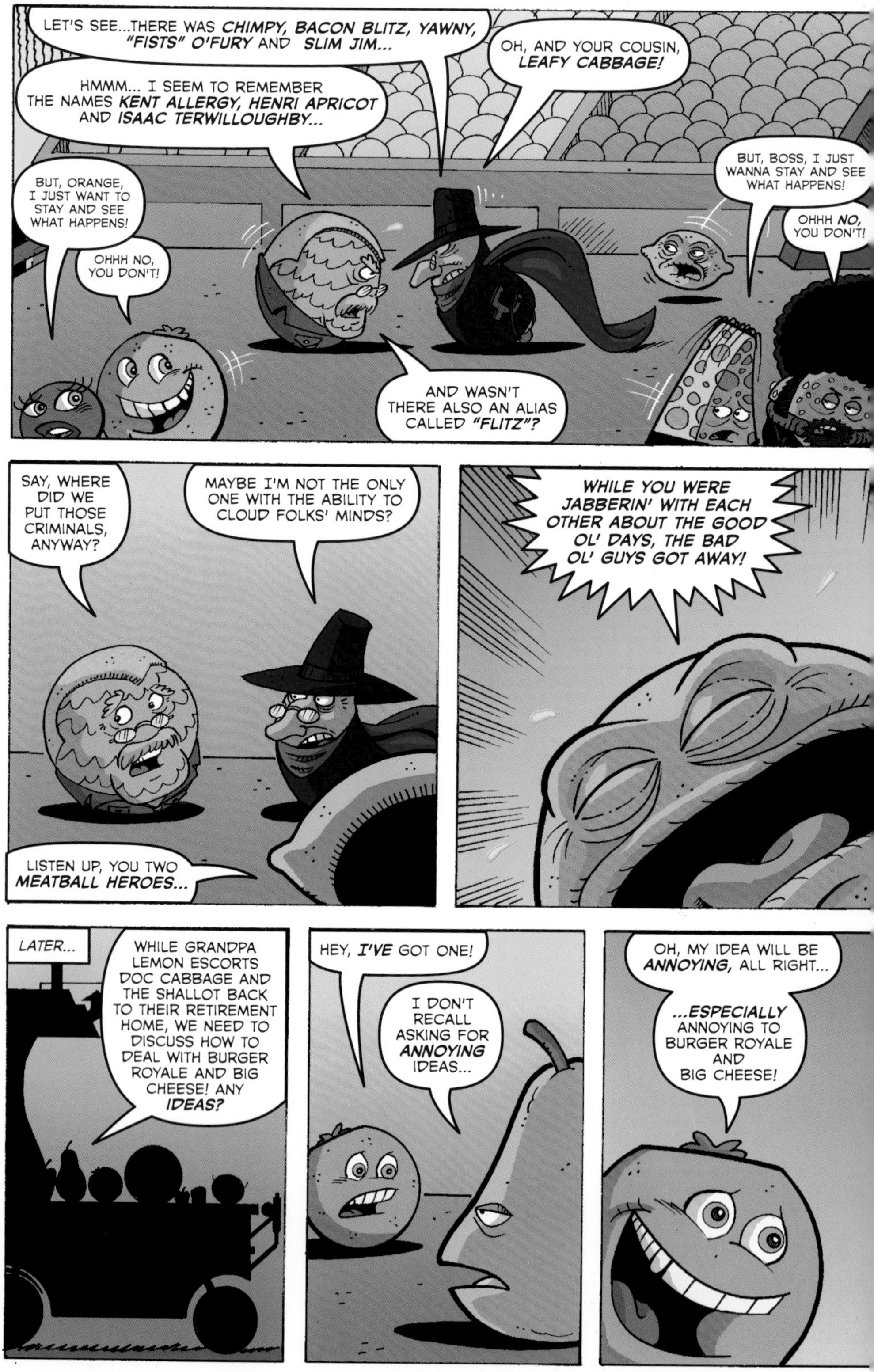
LET'S SEE...THERE WAS CHIMPY, BACON BLITZ, YAWNY, "FISTS" O'FURY AND SLIM JIM...
OH, AND YOUR COUSIN, LEAFY CABBAGE!
HMMM... I SEEM TO REMEMBER THE NAMES KENT ALLERGY, HENRI APRICOT AND ISAAC TERWILLOUGHBY...
BUT, ORANGE, I JUST WANT TO STAY AND SEE WHAT HAPPENS!
OHHH NO, YOU DON'T!
BUT, BOSS, I JUST WANNA STAY AND SEE WHAT HAPPENS!
OHHH NO, YOU DON'T!
AND WASN'T THERE ALSO AN ALIAS CALLED "FLITZ"?
SAY, WHERE DID WE PUT THOSE CRIMINALS, ANYWAY?
MAYBE I'M NOT THE ONLY ONE WITH THE ABILITY TO CLOUD FOLKS' MINDS?
LISTEN UP, YOU TWO MEATBALL HEROES...
WHILE YOU WERE JABBERIN' WITH EACH OTHER ABOUT THE GOOD OL' DAYS, THE BAD OL' GUYS GOT AWAY!
LATER...
WHILE GRANDPA LEMON ESCORTS DOC CABBAGE AND THE SHALLOT BACK TO THEIR RETIREMENT HOME, WE NEED TO DISCUSS HOW TO DEAL WITH BURGER ROYALE AND BIG CHEESE! ANY IDEAS?
HEY, I'VE GOT ONE!
I DON'T RECALL ASKING FOR ANNOYING IDEAS...
OH, MY IDEA WILL BE ANNOYING, ALL RIGHT...
...ESPECIALLY ANNOYING TO BURGER ROYALE AND BIG CHEESE!

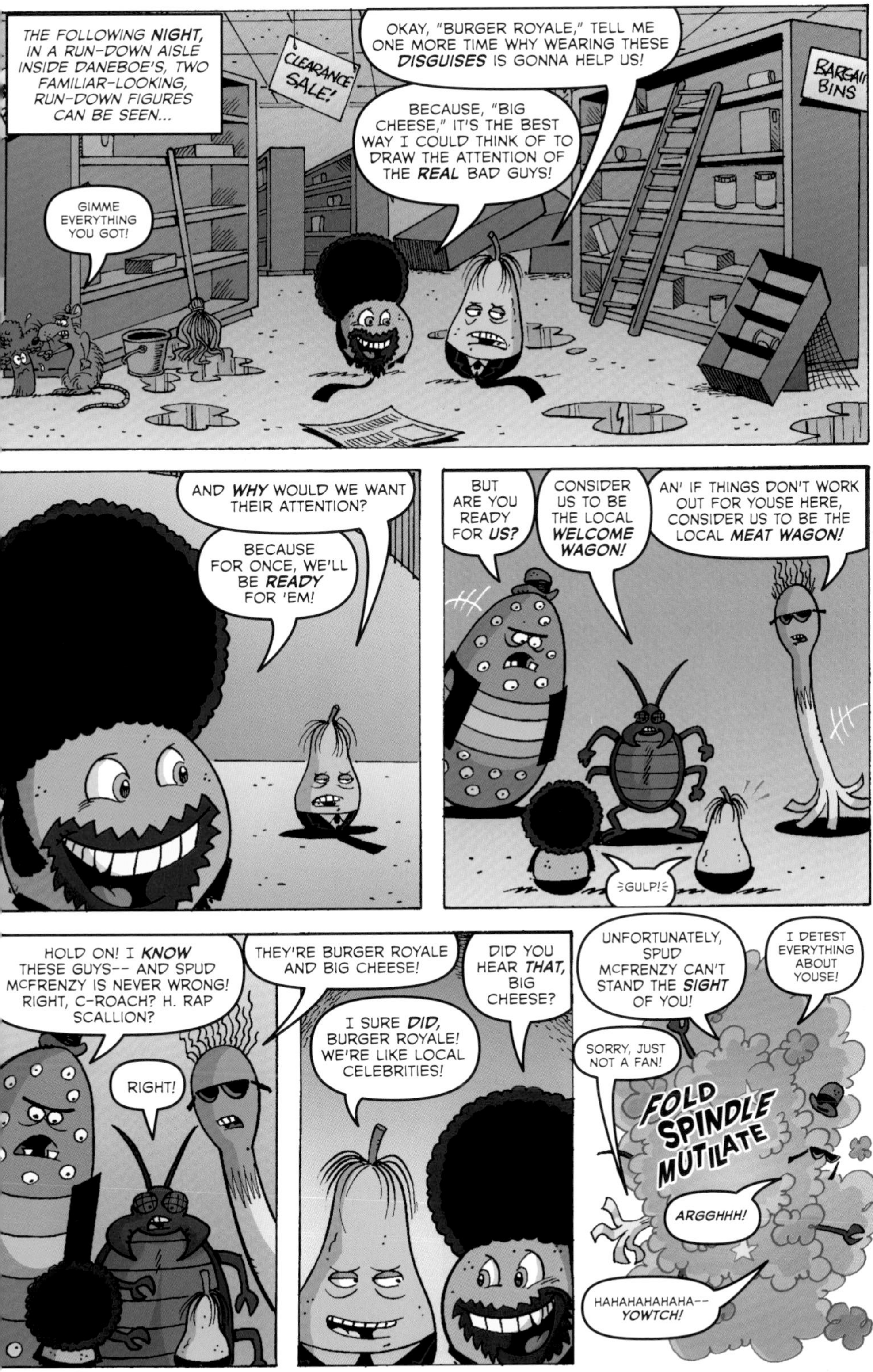
THE FOLLOWING NIGHT, IN A RUN-DOWN AISLE INSIDE DANEBOE'S, TWO FAMILIAR-LOOKING, RUN-DOWN FIGURES CAN BE SEEN...
CLEARANCE SALE!
BARGAIN BINS
OKAY, "BURGER ROYALE," TELL ME ONE MORE TIME WHY WEARING THESE DISGUISES IS GONNA HELP US!
BECAUSE, "BIG CHEESE," IT'S THE BEST WAY I COULD THINK OF TO DRAW THE ATTENTION OF THE REAL BAD GUYS!
GIMME EVERYTHING YOU GOT!
AND WHY WOULD WE WANT THEIR ATTENTION?
BECAUSE FOR ONCE, WE'LL BE READY FOR 'EM!
BUT ARE YOU READY FOR US?
CONSIDER US TO BE THE LOCAL WELCOME WAGON!
AN' IF THINGS DON'T WORK OUT FOR YOUSE HERE, CONSIDER US TO BE THE LOCAL MEAT WAGON!
GULP!
HOLD ON! I KNOW THESE GUYS-- AND SPUD MCFRENZY IS NEVER WRONG! RIGHT, C-ROACH? H. RAP SCALLION?
RIGHT!
THEY'RE BURGER ROYALE AND BIG CHEESE!
DID YOU HEAR THAT, BIG CHEESE?
I SURE DID, BURGER ROYALE! WE'RE LIKE LOCAL CELEBRITIES!
UNFORTUNATELY, SPUD MCFRENZY CAN'T STAND THE SIGHT OF YOU!
I DETEST EVERYTHING ABOUT YOUSE!
SORRY, JUST NOT A FAN!
FOLD SPINDLE MUTILATE
ARGGHHH!
HAHAHAHAHAHA-- YOWTCH!

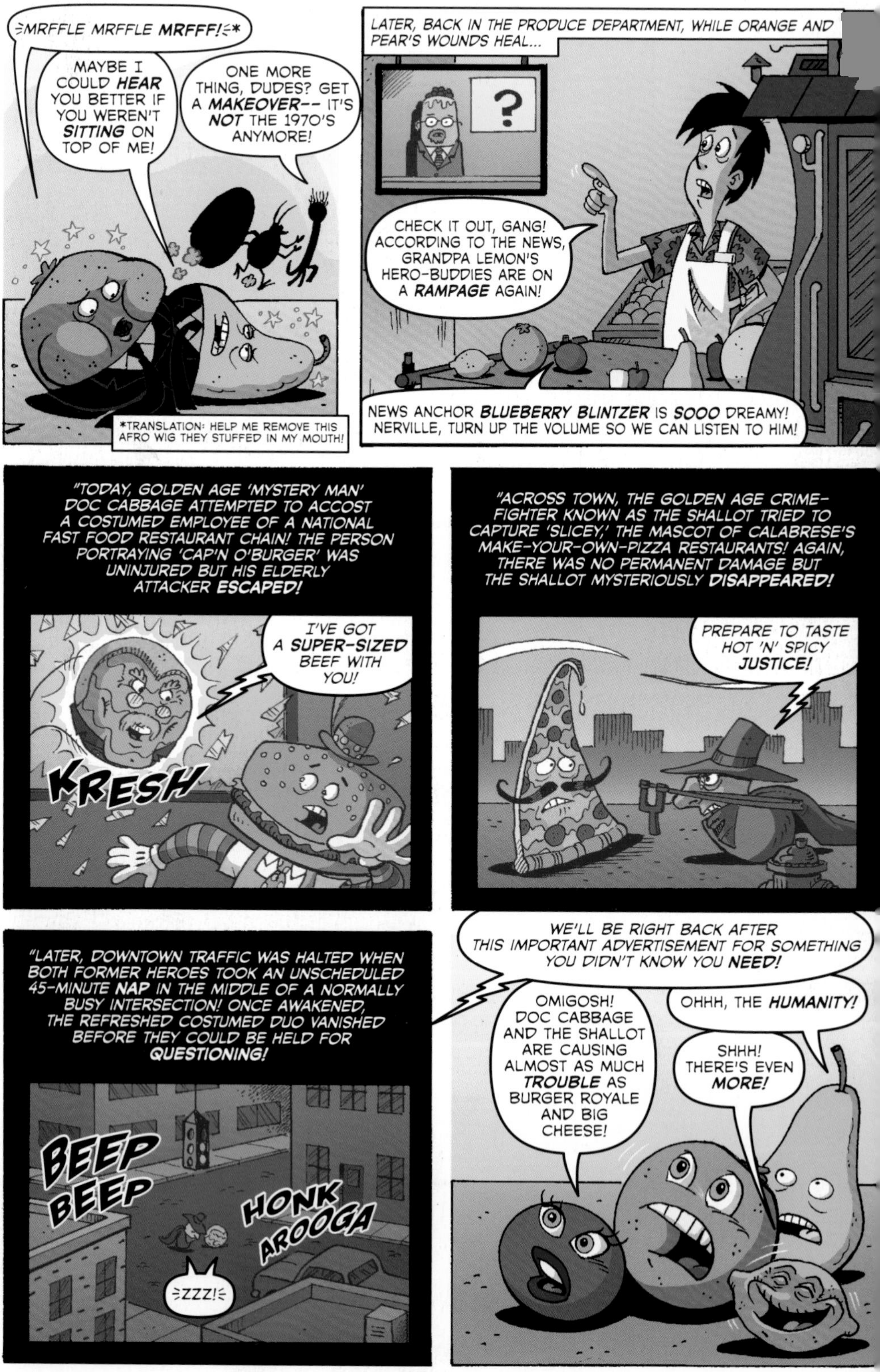

MRFFLE MRFFLE MRFFF!*
MAYBE I COULD HEAR YOU BETTER IF YOU WEREN'T SITTING ON TOP OF ME!
ONE MORE THING, DUDES? GET A MAKEOVER-- IT'S NOT THE 1970'S ANYMORE!
*TRANSLATION: HELP ME REMOVE THIS AFRO WIG THEY STUFFED IN MY MOUTH!
LATER, BACK IN THE PRODUCE DEPARTMENT, WHILE ORANGE AND PEAR'S WOUNDS HEAL...
CHECK IT OUT, GANG! ACCORDING TO THE NEWS, GRANDPA LEMON'S HERO-BUDDIES ARE ON A RAMPAGE AGAIN!
NEWS ANCHOR BLUEBERRY BLINTZER IS SOOO DREAMY! NERVILLE, TURN UP THE VOLUME SO WE CAN LISTEN TO HIM!
"TODAY, GOLDEN AGE 'MYSTERY MAN' DOC CABBAGE ATTEMPTED TO ACCOST A COSTUMED EMPLOYEE OF A NATIONAL FAST FOOD RESTAURANT CHAIN! THE PERSON PORTRAYING 'CAP'N O'BURGER' WAS UNINJURED BUT HIS ELDERLY ATTACKER ESCAPED!
I'VE GOT A SUPER-SIZED BEEF WITH YOU!
KRESH
"ACROSS TOWN, THE GOLDEN AGE CRIME-FIGHTER KNOWN AS THE SHALLOT TRIED TO CAPTURE 'SLICEY,' THE MASCOT OF CALABRESE'S MAKE-YOUR-OWN-PIZZA RESTAURANTS! AGAIN, THERE WAS NO PERMANENT DAMAGE BUT THE SHALLOT MYSTERIOUSLY DISAPPEARED!
PREPARE TO TASTE HOT 'N' SPICY JUSTICE!
"LATER, DOWNTOWN TRAFFIC WAS HALTED WHEN BOTH FORMER HEROES TOOK AN UNSCHEDULED 45-MINUTE NAP IN THE MIDDLE OF A NORMALLY BUSY INTERSECTION! ONCE AWAKENED, THE REFRESHED COSTUMED DUO VANISHED BEFORE THEY COULD BE HELD FOR QUESTIONING!
BEEP BEEP
HONK AROOGA
ZZZ!
WE'LL BE RIGHT BACK AFTER THIS IMPORTANT ADVERTISEMENT FOR SOMETHING YOU DIDN'T KNOW YOU NEED!
OMIGOSH! DOC CABBAGE AND THE SHALLOT ARE CAUSING ALMOST AS MUCH TROUBLE AS BURGER ROYALE AND BIG CHEESE!
OHHH, THE HUMANITY!
SHHH! THERE'S EVEN MORE!

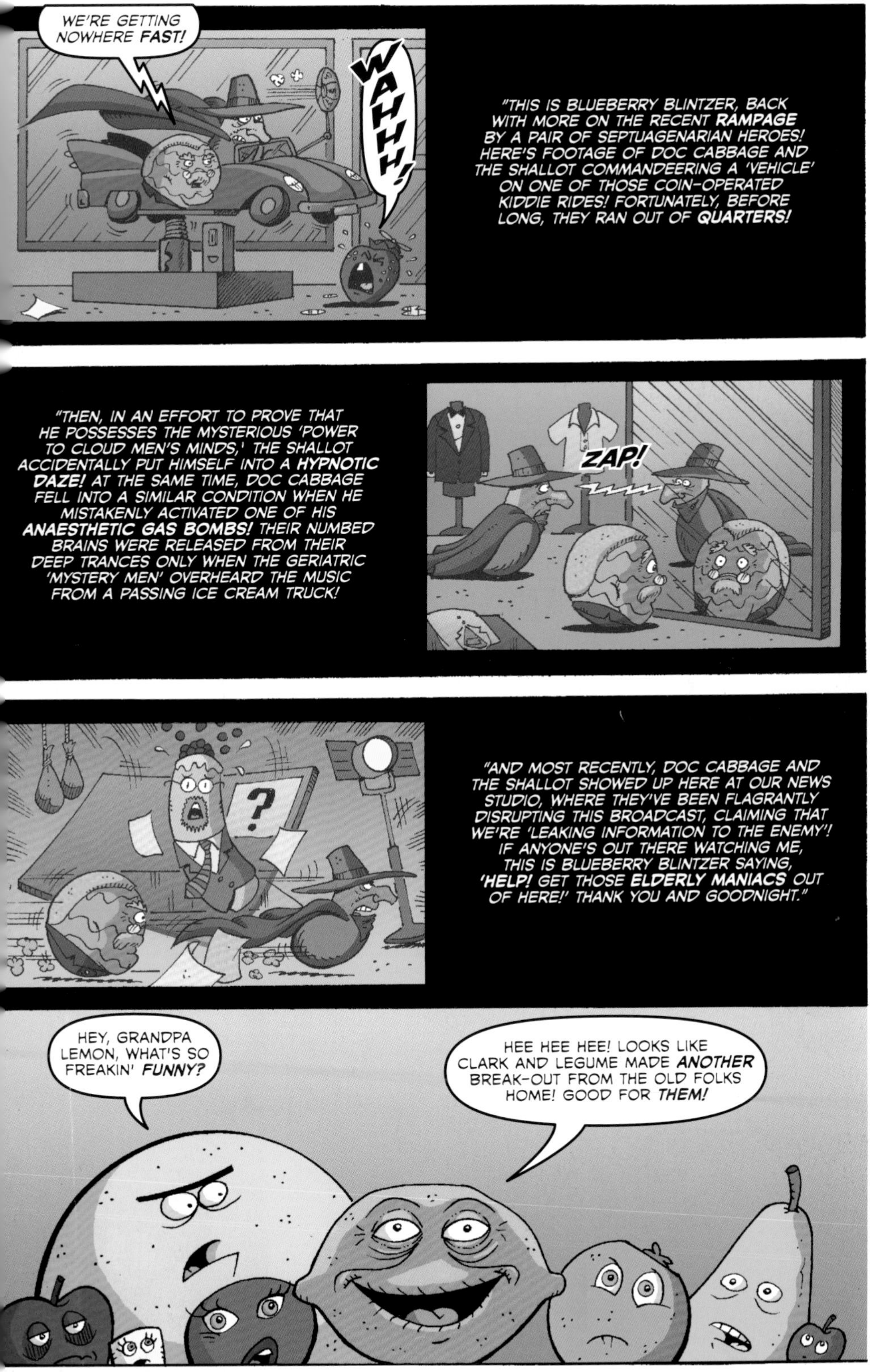
WE'RE GETTING NOWHERE FAST!
WAHHH!
"THIS IS BLUEBERRY BLINTZER, BACK WITH MORE ON THE RECENT RAMPAGE BY A PAIR OF SEPTUAGENARIAN HEROES! HERE'S FOOTAGE OF DOC CABBAGE AND THE SHALLOT COMMANDEERING A 'VEHICLE' ON ONE OF THOSE COIN-OPERATED KIDDIE RIDES! FORTUNATELY, BEFORE LONG, THEY RAN OUT OF QUARTERS!
"THEN, IN AN EFFORT TO PROVE THAT HE POSSESSES THE MYSTERIOUS 'POWER TO CLOUD MEN'S MINDS,' THE SHALLOT ACCIDENTALLY PUT HIMSELF INTO A HYPNOTIC DAZE! AT THE SAME TIME, DOC CABBAGE FELL INTO A SIMILAR CONDITION WHEN HE MISTAKENLY ACTIVATED ONE OF HIS ANAESTHETIC GAS BOMBS! THEIR NUMBED BRAINS WERE RELEASED FROM THEIR DEEP TRANCES ONLY WHEN THE GERIATRIC 'MYSTERY MEN' OVERHEARD THE MUSIC FROM A PASSING ICE CREAM TRUCK!
ZAP!
?
"AND MOST RECENTLY, DOC CABBAGE AND THE SHALLOT SHOWED UP HERE AT OUR NEWS STUDIO, WHERE THEY'VE BEEN FLAGRANTLY DISRUPTING THIS BROADCAST, CLAIMING THAT WE'RE 'LEAKING INFORMATION TO THE ENEMY'! IF ANYONE'S OUT THERE WATCHING ME, THIS IS BLUEBERRY BLINTZER SAYING, 'HELP! GET THOSE ELDERLY MANIACS OUT OF HERE!' THANK YOU AND GOODNIGHT."
HEY, GRANDPA LEMON, WHAT'S SO FREAKIN' FUNNY?
HEE HEE HEE! LOOKS LIKE CLARK AND LEGUME MADE ANOTHER BREAK-OUT FROM THE OLD FOLKS HOME! GOOD FOR THEM!

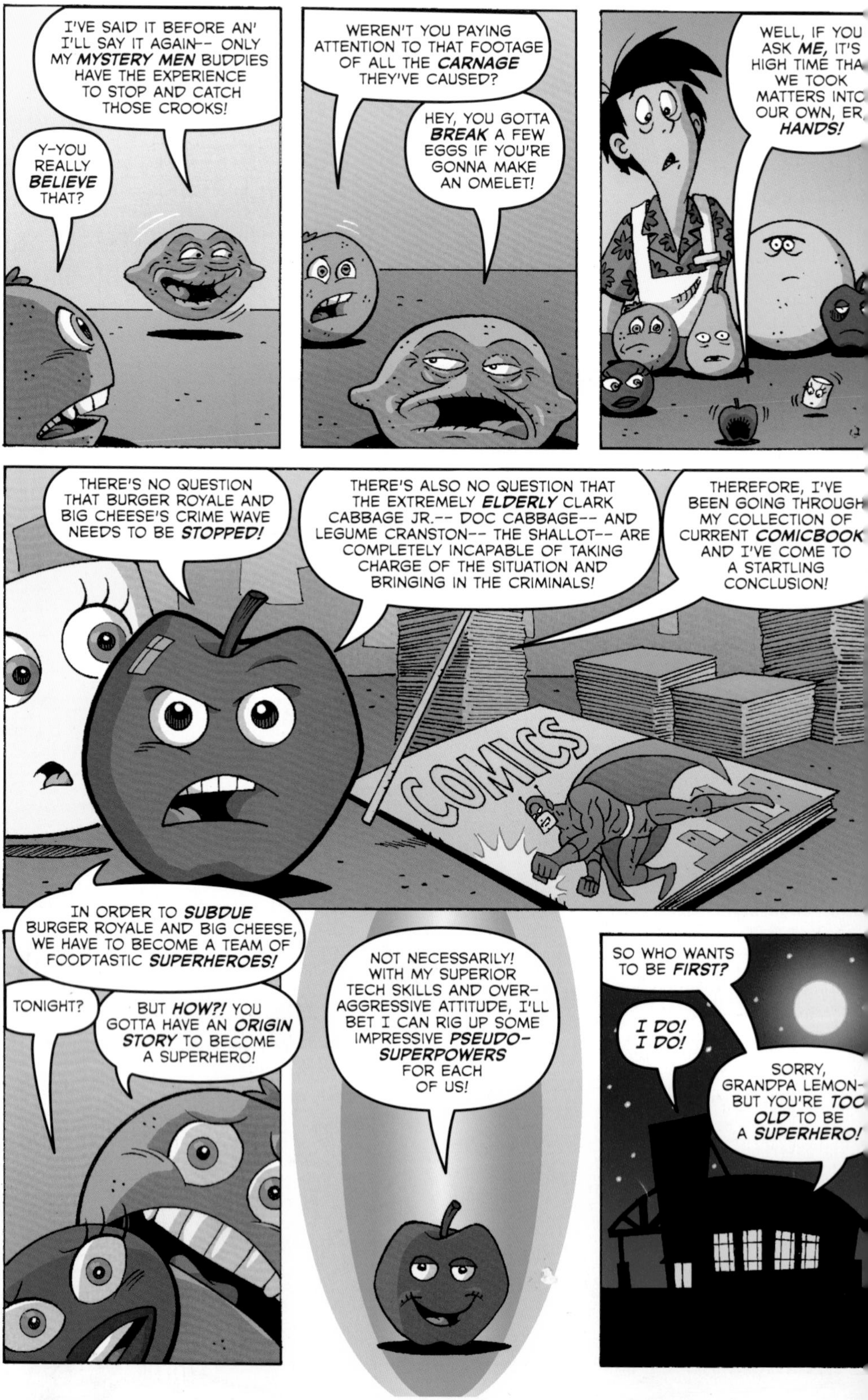
I'VE SAID IT BEFORE AN' I'LL SAY IT AGAIN-- ONLY MY MYSTERY MEN BUDDIES HAVE THE EXPERIENCE TO STOP AND CATCH THOSE CROOKS!
Y-YOU REALLY BELIEVE THAT?
WEREN'T YOU PAYING ATTENTION TO THAT FOOTAGE OF ALL THE CARNAGE THEY'VE CAUSED?
HEY, YOU GOTTA BREAK A FEW EGGS IF YOU'RE GONNA MAKE AN OMELET!
WELL, IF YOU ASK ME, IT'S HIGH TIME THA WE TOOK MATTERS INTO OUR OWN, ER, HANDS!
THERE'S NO QUESTION THAT BURGER ROYALE AND BIG CHEESE'S CRIME WAVE NEEDS TO BE STOPPED!
THERE'S ALSO NO QUESTION THAT THE EXTREMELY ELDERLY CLARK CABBAGE JR.-- DOC CABBAGE-- AND LEGUME CRANSTON-- THE SHALLOT-- ARE COMPLETELY INCAPABLE OF TAKING CHARGE OF THE SITUATION AND BRINGING IN THE CRIMINALS!
THEREFORE, I'VE BEEN GOING THROUGH MY COLLECTION OF CURRENT COMICBOOK AND I'VE COME TO A STARTLING CONCLUSION!
COMICS
IN ORDER TO SUBDUE BURGER ROYALE AND BIG CHEESE, WE HAVE TO BECOME A TEAM OF FOODTASTIC SUPERHEROES!
TONIGHT?
BUT HOW?! YOU GOTTA HAVE AN ORIGIN STORY TO BECOME A SUPERHERO!
NOT NECESSARILY! WITH MY SUPERIOR TECH SKILLS AND OVER-AGGRESSIVE ATTITUDE, I'LL BET I CAN RIG UP SOME IMPRESSIVE PSEUDO-SUPERPOWERS FOR EACH OF US!
SO WHO WANTS TO BE FIRST?
I DO! I DO!
SORRY, GRANDPA LEMON-BUT YOU'RE TOO OLD TO BE A SUPERHERO!

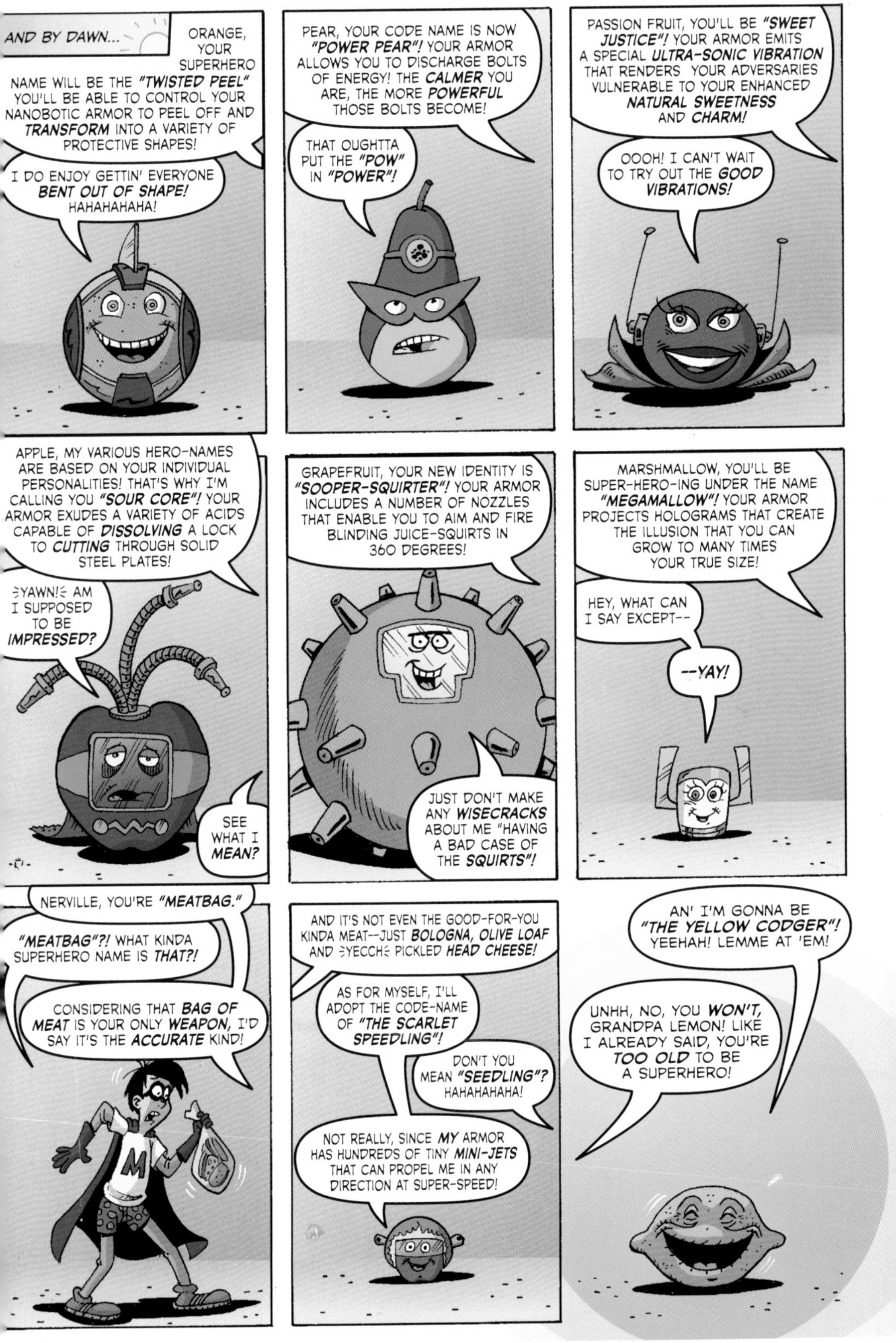
AND BY DAWN...
ORANGE, YOUR SUPERHERO NAME WILL BE THE "TWISTED PEEL" YOU'LL BE ABLE TO CONTROL YOUR NANOBOTIC ARMOR TO PEEL OFF AND TRANSFORM INTO A VARIETY OF PROTECTIVE SHAPES!
I DO ENJOY GETTIN' EVERYONE BENT OUT OF SHAPE! HAHAHAHAHA!
PEAR, YOUR CODE NAME IS NOW "POWER PEAR"! YOUR ARMOR ALLOWS YOU TO DISCHARGE BOLTS OF ENERGY! THE CALMER YOU ARE, THE MORE POWERFUL THOSE BOLTS BECOME!
THAT OUGHTTA PUT THE "POW" IN "POWER"!
PASSION FRUIT, YOU'LL BE "SWEET JUSTICE"! YOUR ARMOR EMITS A SPECIAL ULTRA-SONIC VIBRATION THAT RENDERS YOUR ADVERSARIES VULNERABLE TO YOUR ENHANCED NATURAL SWEETNESS AND CHARM!
OOOH! I CAN'T WAIT TO TRY OUT THE GOOD VIBRATIONS!
APPLE, MY VARIOUS HERO-NAMES ARE BASED ON YOUR INDIVIDUAL PERSONALITIES! THAT'S WHY I'M CALLING YOU "SOUR CORE"! YOUR ARMOR EXUDES A VARIETY OF ACIDS CAPABLE OF DISSOLVING A LOCK TO CUTTING THROUGH SOLID STEEL PLATES!
YAWN! AM I SUPPOSED TO BE IMPRESSED?
SEE WHAT I MEAN?
GRAPEFRUIT, YOUR NEW IDENTITY IS "SOOPER-SQUIRTER"! YOUR ARMOR INCLUDES A NUMBER OF NOZZLES THAT ENABLE YOU TO AIM AND FIRE BLINDING JUICE-SQUIRTS IN 360 DEGREES!
JUST DON'T MAKE ANY WISECRACKS ABOUT ME "HAVING A BAD CASE OF THE SQUIRTS"!
MARSHMALLOW, YOU'LL BE SUPER-HERO-ING UNDER THE NAME "MEGAMALLOW"! YOUR ARMOR PROJECTS HOLOGRAMS THAT CREATE THE ILLUSION THAT YOU CAN GROW TO MANY TIMES YOUR TRUE SIZE!
HEY, WHAT CAN I SAY EXCEPT--
--YAY!
NERVILLE, YOU'RE "MEATBAG."
"MEATBAG"?! WHAT KINDA SUPERHERO NAME IS THAT?!
CONSIDERING THAT BAG OF MEAT IS YOUR ONLY WEAPON, I'D SAY IT'S THE ACCURATE KIND!
AND IT'S NOT EVEN THE GOOD-FOR-YOU KINDA MEAT--JUST BOLOGNA, OLIVE LOAF AND YECCH PICKLED HEAD CHEESE!
AS FOR MYSELF, I'LL ADOPT THE CODE-NAME OF "THE SCARLET SPEEDLING"!
DON'T YOU MEAN "SEEDLING"? HAHAHAHAHA!
NOT REALLY, SINCE MY ARMOR HAS HUNDREDS OF TINY MINI-JETS THAT CAN PROPEL ME IN ANY DIRECTION AT SUPER-SPEED!
AN' I'M GONNA BE "THE YELLOW CODGER"! YEEHAH! LEMME AT 'EM!
UNHH, NO, YOU WON'T, GRANDPA LEMON! LIKE I ALREADY SAID, YOU'RE TOO OLD TO BE A SUPERHERO!

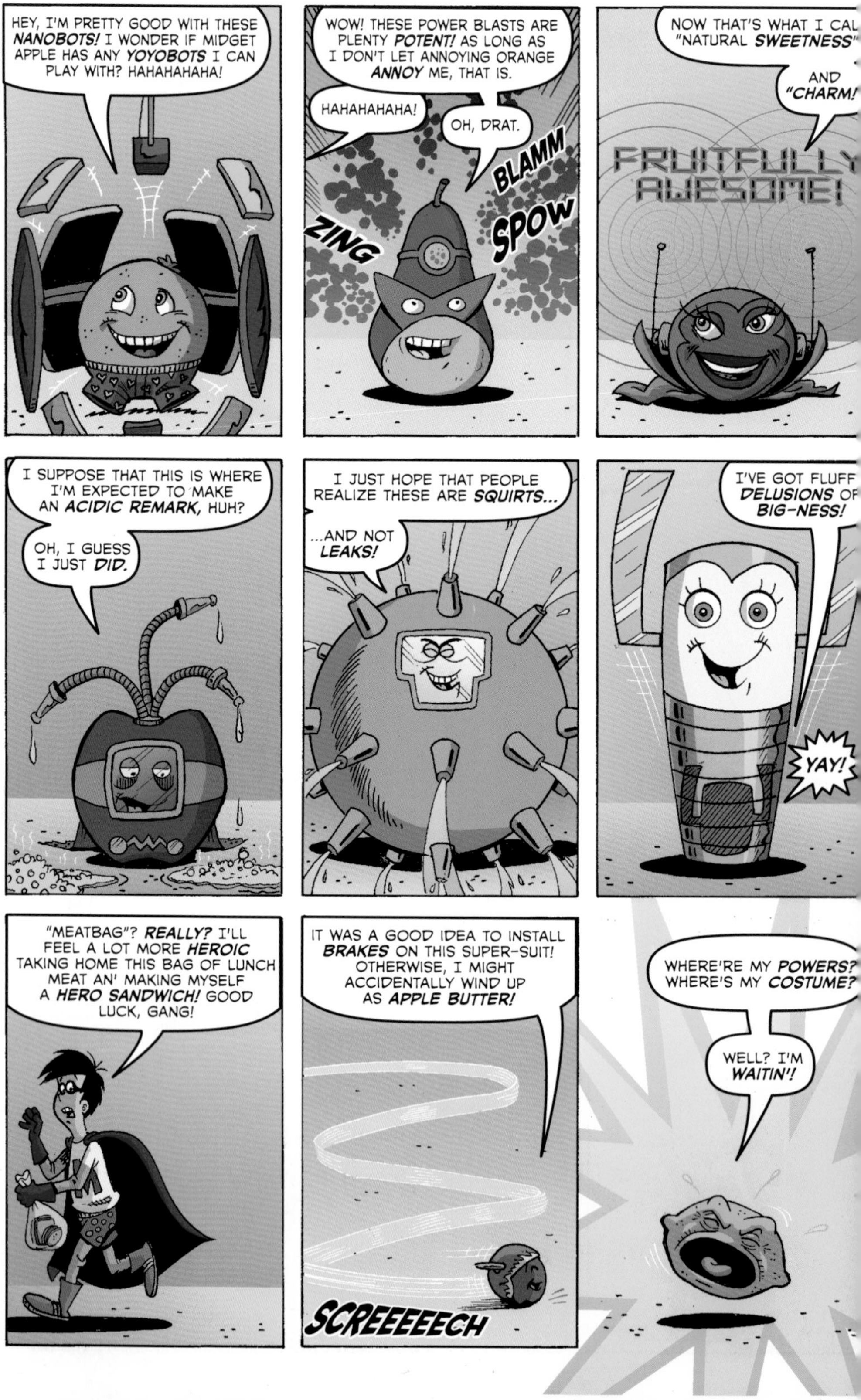
HEY, I'M PRETTY GOOD WITH THESE NANOBOTS! I WONDER IF MIDGET APPLE HAS ANY YOYOBOTS I CAN PLAY WITH? HAHAHAHAHA!
WOW! THESE POWER BLASTS ARE PLENTY POTENT! AS LONG AS I DON'T LET ANNOYING ORANGE ANNOY ME, THAT IS.
HAHAHAHAHA!
OH, DRAT.
BLAMM
ZING
SPOW
NOW THAT'S WHAT I CAL
"NATURAL SWEETNESS"
AND "CHARM!
FRUITFULLY AWESOME!
I SUPPOSE THAT THIS IS WHERE I'M EXPECTED TO MAKE AN ACIDIC REMARK, HUH?
OH, I GUESS I JUST DID.
I JUST HOPE THAT PEOPLE REALIZE THESE ARE SQUIRTS...
...AND NOT LEAKS!
I'VE GOT FLUFF DELUSIONS OF BIG-NESS!
YAY!
"MEATBAG"? REALLY? I'LL FEEL A LOT MORE HEROIC TAKING HOME THIS BAG OF LUNCH MEAT AN' MAKING MYSELF A HERO SANDWICH! GOOD LUCK, GANG!
IT WAS A GOOD IDEA TO INSTALL BRAKES ON THIS SUPER-SUIT! OTHERWISE, I MIGHT ACCIDENTALLY WIND UP AS APPLE BUTTER!
SCREEEEEECH
WHERE'RE MY POWERS? WHERE'S MY COSTUME?
WELL? I'M WAITIN'!

THAT NIGHT...

OKAY, TEAM, OUR *FIRST MISSION* IS TO SEARCH FOR AND APPREHEND BURGER ROYALE AND BIG CHEESE!

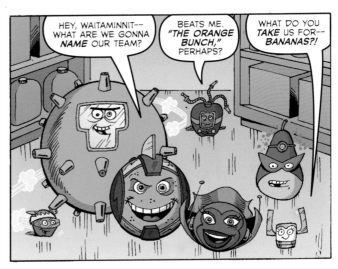

HEY, WAITAMINNIT-- WHAT ARE WE GONNA *NAME* OUR TEAM?

BEATS ME. *"THE ORANGE BUNCH,"* PERHAPS?

WHAT DO YOU *TAKE* US FOR-- *BANANAS?!*

SUDDENLY...

ARGGH!

I GUESS THIS IS WHAT WE DESERVE FOR GETTING TOO CLOSE TO THE STORE'S *PET DEPARTMENT!*

≥HISSSSS!≤

≥GULP!≤

≥EWW!≤ THAT ESCAPED SNAKE JUST *SWALLOWED* APPLE... I MEAN, SOUR CORE!

EHH... SERVES 'IM *RIGHT* FOR THAT DOPEY "BANANA BUNCH" SUGGESTION...

HEY, I KNOW! HOW ABOUT... *THE EDIBLES?* KINDA LIKE *THE INCREDIBLES* BUT WITHOUT THE *"INCR"* PART!

AS FOR THAT POOR SNAKE, A FEW *ANTI-ACID* TABLETS OUGHTTA SET 'IM *STRAIGHT* IN *NO* TIME!

≥BLURP!≤

HEY, I'M OPEN TO *SUGGESTIONS!*

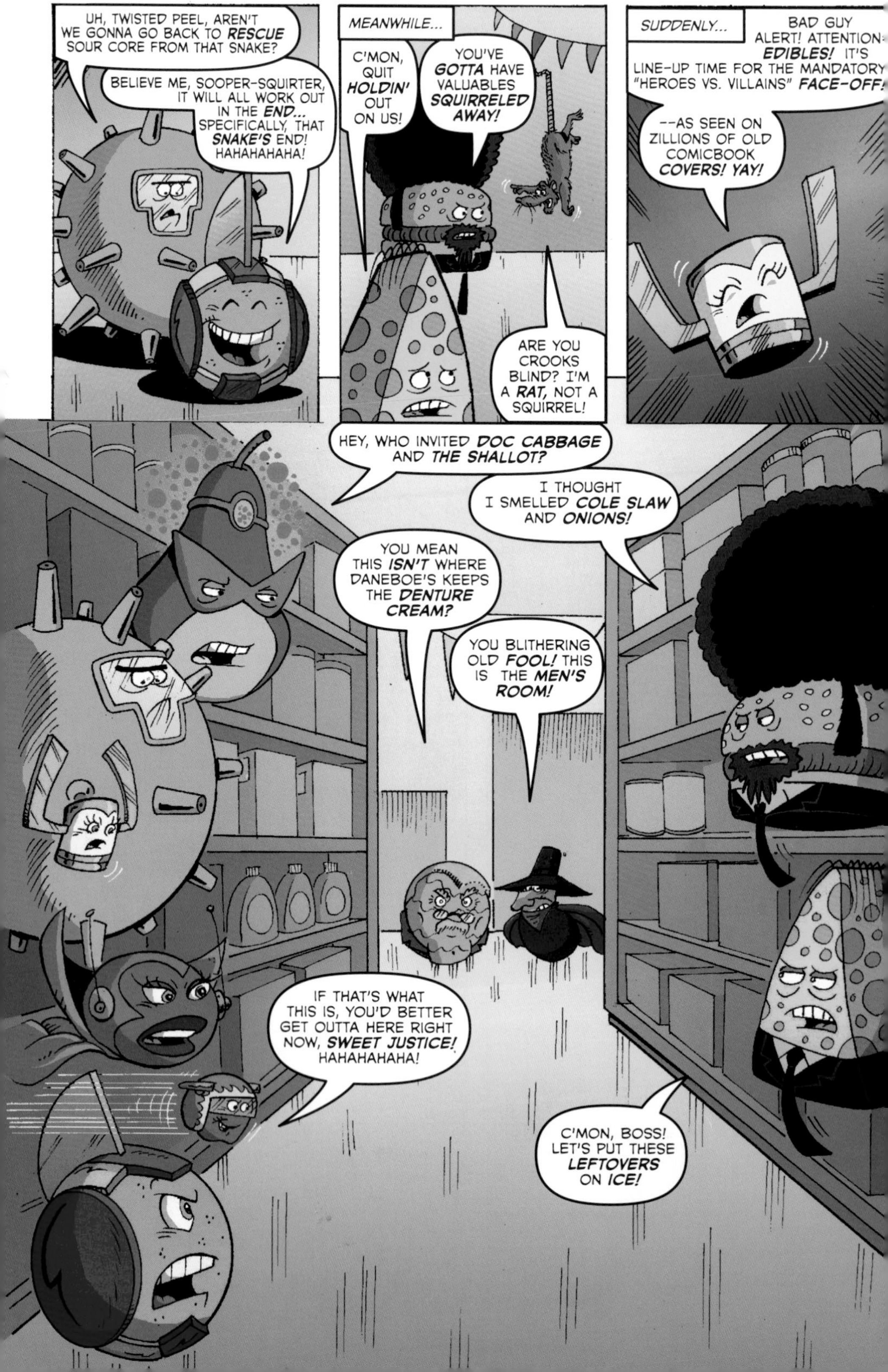
UH, TWISTED PEEL, AREN'T WE GONNA GO BACK TO RESCUE SOUR CORE FROM THAT SNAKE?
BELIEVE ME, SOOPER-SQUIRTER, IT WILL ALL WORK OUT IN THE END... SPECIFICALLY, THAT SNAKE'S END! HAHAHAHAHA!
MEANWHILE...
C'MON, QUIT HOLDIN' OUT ON US!
YOU'VE GOTTA HAVE VALUABLES SQUIRRELED AWAY!
ARE YOU CROOKS BLIND? I'M A RAT, NOT A SQUIRREL!
SUDDENLY...
BAD GUY ALERT! ATTENTION: EDIBLES! IT'S LINE-UP TIME FOR THE MANDATORY "HEROES VS. VILLAINS" FACE-OFF!
--AS SEEN ON ZILLIONS OF OLD COMICBOOK COVERS! YAY!
HEY, WHO INVITED DOC CABBAGE AND THE SHALLOT?
I THOUGHT I SMELLED COLE SLAW AND ONIONS!
YOU MEAN THIS ISN'T WHERE DANEBOE'S KEEPS THE DENTURE CREAM?
YOU BLITHERING OLD FOOL! THIS IS THE MEN'S ROOM!
IF THAT'S WHAT THIS IS, YOU'D BETTER GET OUTTA HERE RIGHT NOW, SWEET JUSTICE! HAHAHAHAHA!
C'MON, BOSS! LET'S PUT THESE LEFTOVERS ON ICE!

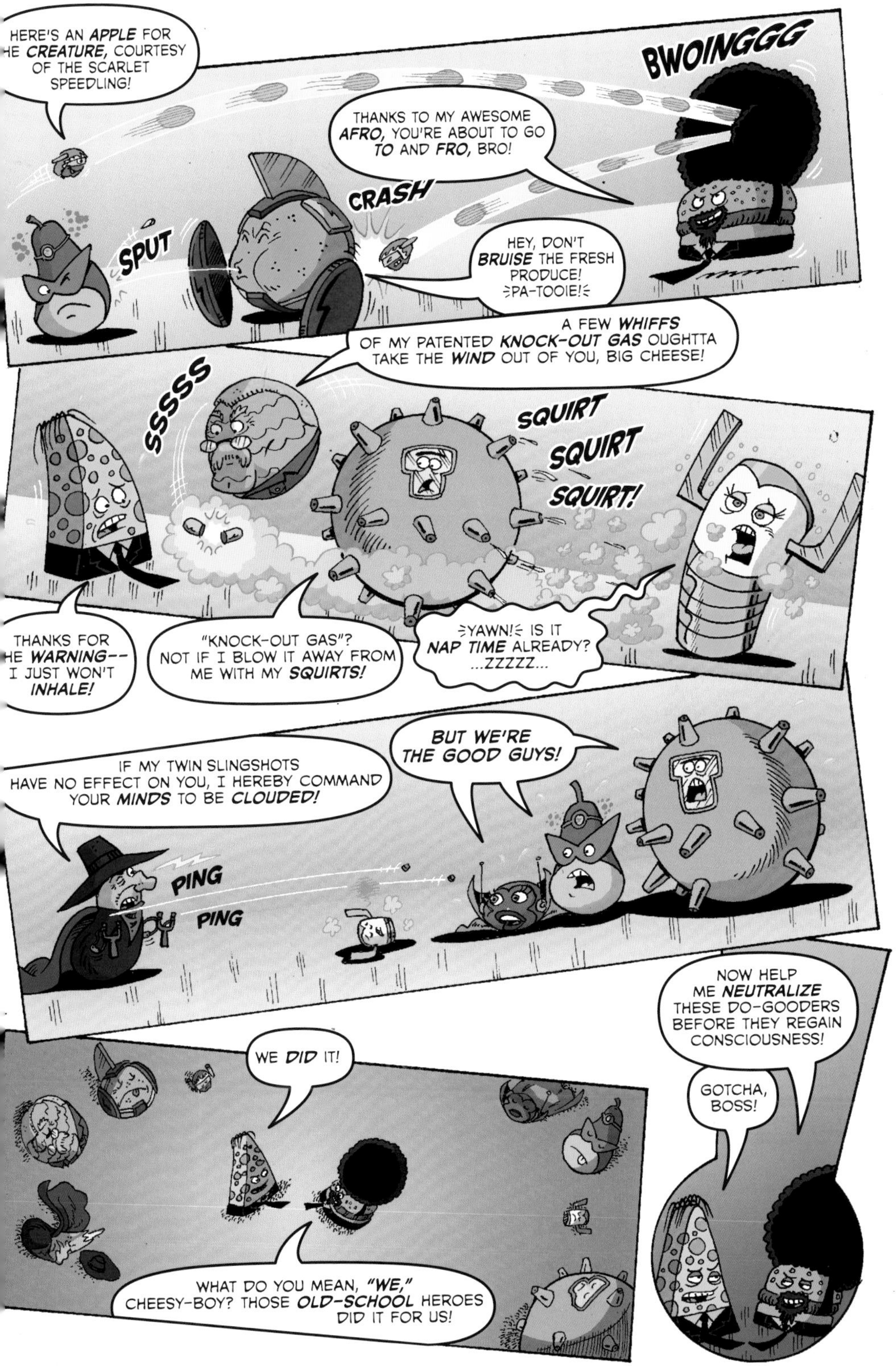
HERE'S AN APPLE FOR HE CREATURE, COURTESY OF THE SCARLET SPEEDLING!
BWOINGGG
THANKS TO MY AWESOME AFRO, YOU'RE ABOUT TO GO TO AND FRO, BRO!
CRASH
SPUT
HEY, DON'T BRUISE THE FRESH PRODUCE! ⋝PA-TOOIE!⋜
A FEW WHIFFS OF MY PATENTED KNOCK-OUT GAS OUGHTTA TAKE THE WIND OUT OF YOU, BIG CHEESE!
SSSSS
SQUIRT
SQUIRT
SQUIRT!
THANKS FOR HE WARNING-- I JUST WON'T INHALE!
"KNOCK-OUT GAS"? NOT IF I BLOW IT AWAY FROM ME WITH MY SQUIRTS!
⋝YAWN!⋜ IS IT NAP TIME ALREADY? ...ZZZZZ...
IF MY TWIN SLINGSHOTS HAVE NO EFFECT ON YOU, I HEREBY COMMAND YOUR MINDS TO BE CLOUDED!
BUT WE'RE THE GOOD GUYS!
PING
PING
WE DID IT!
WHAT DO YOU MEAN, "WE," CHEESY-BOY? THOSE OLD-SCHOOL HEROES DID IT FOR US!
NOW HELP ME NEUTRALIZE THESE DO-GOODERS BEFORE THEY REGAIN CONSCIOUSNESS!
GOTCHA, BOSS!

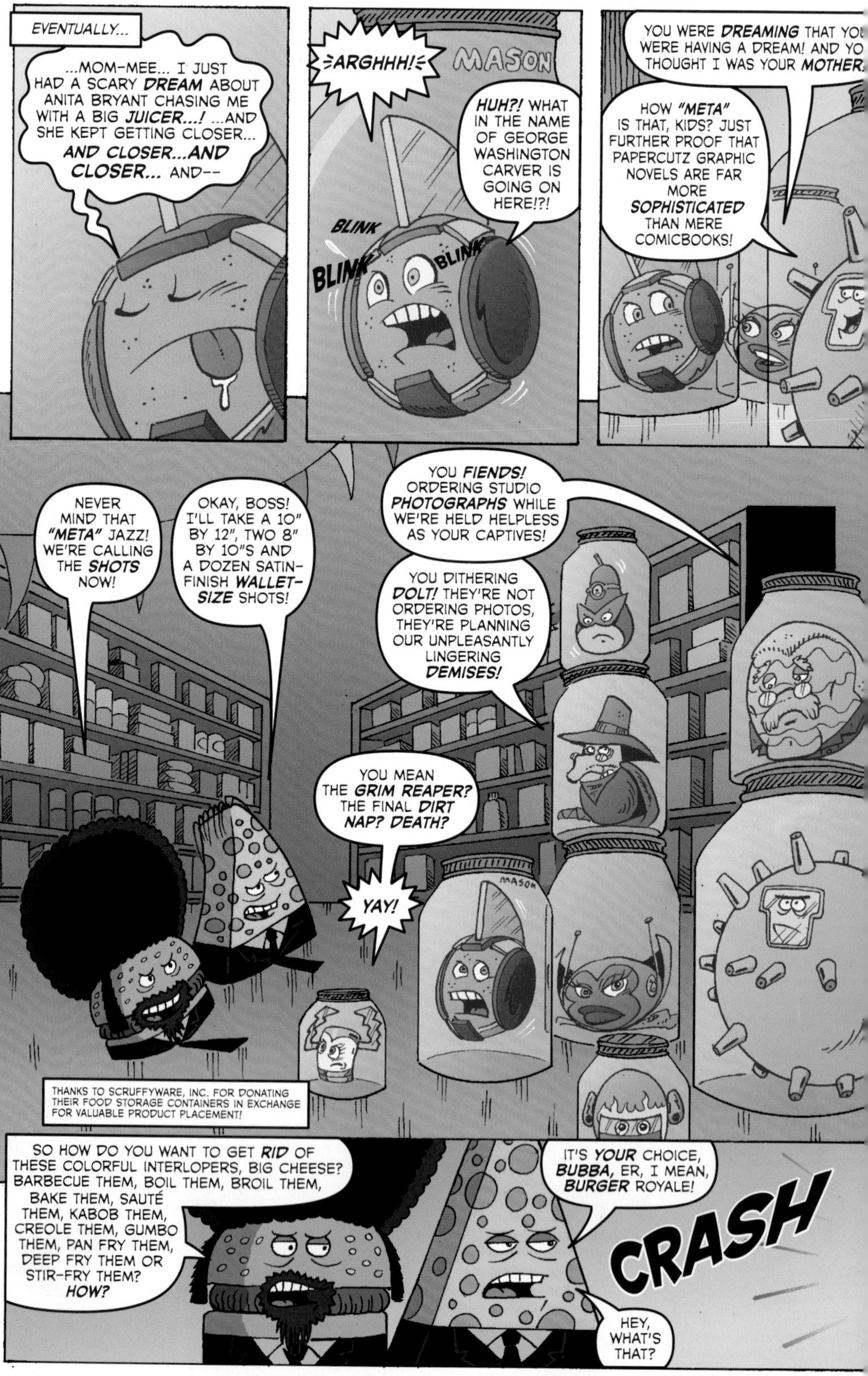
EVENTUALLY...
...MOM-MEE... I JUST HAD A SCARY DREAM ABOUT ANITA BRYANT CHASING ME WITH A BIG JUICER...! ...AND SHE KEPT GETTING CLOSER... AND CLOSER...AND CLOSER... AND--
ARGHHH!
MASON
HUH?! WHAT IN THE NAME OF GEORGE WASHINGTON CARVER IS GOING ON HERE!?!
BLINK
BLINK
BLINK
YOU WERE DREAMING THAT YOU WERE HAVING A DREAM! AND YOU THOUGHT I WAS YOUR MOTHER!
HOW "META" IS THAT, KIDS? JUST FURTHER PROOF THAT PAPERCUTZ GRAPHIC NOVELS ARE FAR MORE SOPHISTICATED THAN MERE COMICBOOKS!
NEVER MIND THAT "META" JAZZ! WE'RE CALLING THE SHOTS NOW!
OKAY, BOSS! I'LL TAKE A 10" BY 12", TWO 8" BY 10"S AND A DOZEN SATIN-FINISH WALLET-SIZE SHOTS!
YOU FIENDS! ORDERING STUDIO PHOTOGRAPHS WHILE WE'RE HELD HELPLESS AS YOUR CAPTIVES!
YOU DITHERING DOLT! THEY'RE NOT ORDERING PHOTOS, THEY'RE PLANNING OUR UNPLEASANTLY LINGERING DEMISES!
YOU MEAN THE GRIM REAPER? THE FINAL DIRT NAP? DEATH?
YAY!
MASON
THANKS TO SCRUFFYWARE, INC. FOR DONATING THEIR FOOD STORAGE CONTAINERS IN EXCHANGE FOR VALUABLE PRODUCT PLACEMENT!
SO HOW DO YOU WANT TO GET RID OF THESE COLORFUL INTERLOPERS, BIG CHEESE? BARBECUE THEM, BOIL THEM, BROIL THEM, BAKE THEM, SAUTÉ THEM, KABOB THEM, CREOLE THEM, GUMBO THEM, PAN FRY THEM, DEEP FRY THEM OR STIR-FRY THEM? HOW?
IT'S YOUR CHOICE, BUBBA, ER, I MEAN, BURGER ROYALE!
CRASH
HEY, WHAT'S THAT?

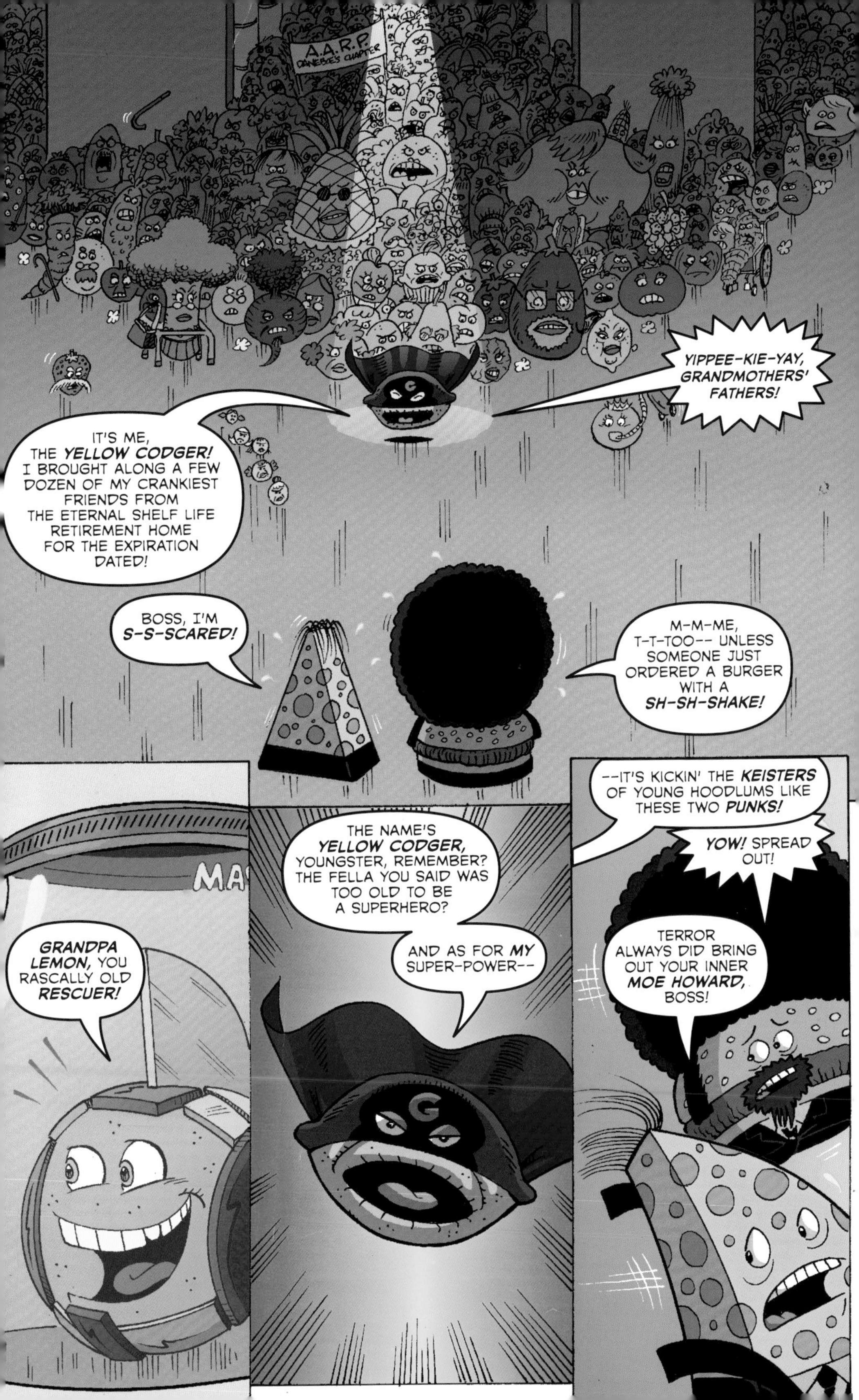
A.A.R.P.
YIPPEE-KIE-YAY, GRANDMOTHERS' FATHERS!
IT'S ME, THE YELLOW CODGER! I BROUGHT ALONG A FEW DOZEN OF MY CRANKIEST FRIENDS FROM THE ETERNAL SHELF LIFE RETIREMENT HOME FOR THE EXPIRATION DATED!
BOSS, I'M S-S-SCARED!
M-M-ME, T-T-TOO-- UNLESS SOMEONE JUST ORDERED A BURGER WITH A SH-SH-SHAKE!
GRANDPA LEMON, YOU RASCALLY OLD RESCUER!
THE NAME'S YELLOW CODGER, YOUNGSTER, REMEMBER? THE FELLA YOU SAID WAS TOO OLD TO BE A SUPERHERO?
AND AS FOR MY SUPER-POWER--
--IT'S KICKIN' THE KEISTERS OF YOUNG HOODLUMS LIKE THESE TWO PUNKS!
YOW! SPREAD OUT!
TERROR ALWAYS DID BRING OUT YOUR INNER MOE HOWARD, BOSS!

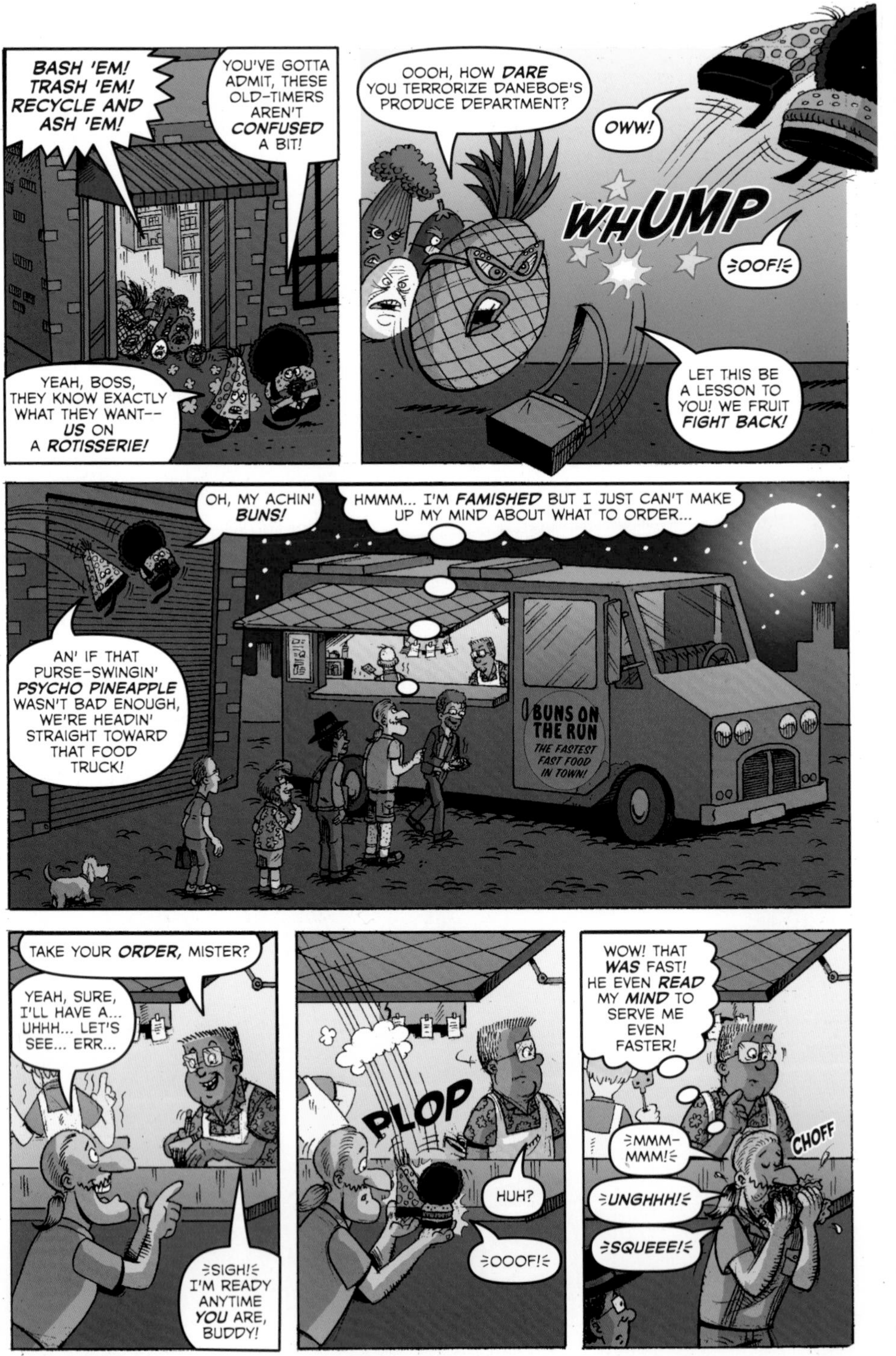
BASH 'EM! TRASH 'EM! RECYCLE AND ASH 'EM!
YOU'VE GOTTA ADMIT, THESE OLD-TIMERS AREN'T CONFUSED A BIT!
YEAH, BOSS, THEY KNOW EXACTLY WHAT THEY WANT-- US ON A ROTISSERIE!
OOOH, HOW DARE YOU TERRORIZE DANEBOE'S PRODUCE DEPARTMENT?
OWW!
WHUMP
OOF!
LET THIS BE A LESSON TO YOU! WE FRUIT FIGHT BACK!
OH, MY ACHIN' BUNS!
HMMM... I'M FAMISHED BUT I JUST CAN'T MAKE UP MY MIND ABOUT WHAT TO ORDER...
AN' IF THAT PURSE-SWINGIN' PSYCHO PINEAPPLE WASN'T BAD ENOUGH, WE'RE HEADIN' STRAIGHT TOWARD THAT FOOD TRUCK!
BUNS ON THE RUN
THE FASTEST FAST FOOD IN TOWN!
TAKE YOUR ORDER, MISTER?
YEAH, SURE, I'LL HAVE A... UHHH... LET'S SEE... ERR...
SIGH! I'M READY ANYTIME YOU ARE, BUDDY!
PLOP
HUH?
OOOF!
WOW! THAT WAS FAST! HE EVEN READ MY MIND TO SERVE ME EVEN FASTER!
CHOFF
MMM-MMM!
UNGHHH!
SQUEEE!

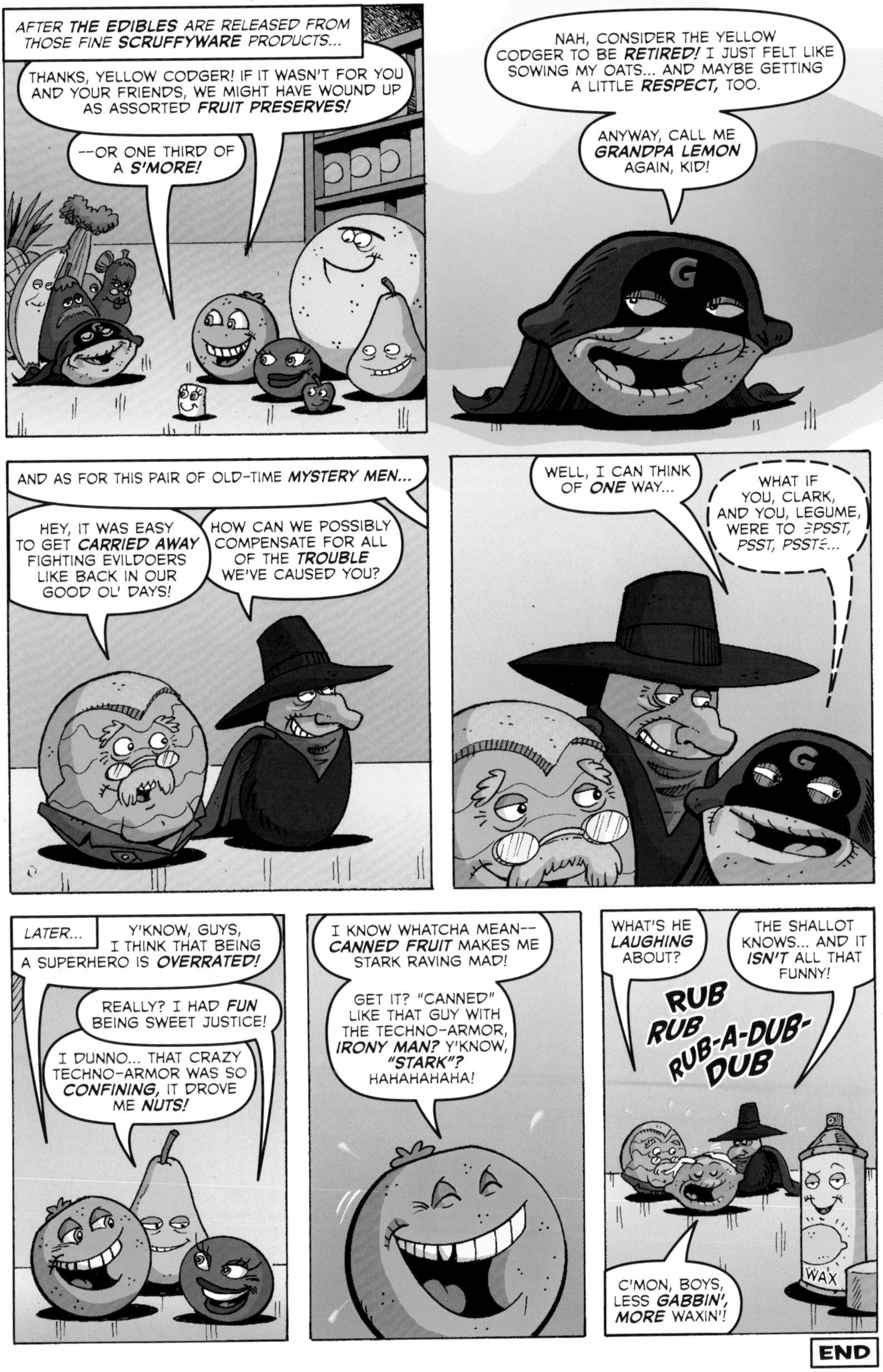
AFTER THE EDIBLES ARE RELEASED FROM THOSE FINE SCRUFFYWARE PRODUCTS...
THANKS, YELLOW CODGER! IF IT WASN'T FOR YOU AND YOUR FRIENDS, WE MIGHT HAVE WOUND UP AS ASSORTED FRUIT PRESERVES!
--OR ONE THIRD OF A S'MORE!
NAH, CONSIDER THE YELLOW CODGER TO BE RETIRED! I JUST FELT LIKE SOWING MY OATS... AND MAYBE GETTING A LITTLE RESPECT, TOO.
ANYWAY, CALL ME GRANDPA LEMON AGAIN, KID!
AND AS FOR THIS PAIR OF OLD-TIME MYSTERY MEN...
HEY, IT WAS EASY TO GET CARRIED AWAY FIGHTING EVILDOERS LIKE BACK IN OUR GOOD OL' DAYS!
HOW CAN WE POSSIBLY COMPENSATE FOR ALL OF THE TROUBLE WE'VE CAUSED YOU?
WELL, I CAN THINK OF ONE WAY...
WHAT IF YOU, CLARK, AND YOU, LEGUME, WERE TO ≶PSST, PSST, PSST≶...
LATER...
Y'KNOW, GUYS, I THINK THAT BEING A SUPERHERO IS OVERRATED!
REALLY? I HAD FUN BEING SWEET JUSTICE!
I DUNNO... THAT CRAZY TECHNO-ARMOR WAS SO CONFINING, IT DROVE ME NUTS!
I KNOW WHATCHA MEAN-- CANNED FRUIT MAKES ME STARK RAVING MAD!
GET IT? "CANNED" LIKE THAT GUY WITH THE TECHNO-ARMOR, IRONY MAN? Y'KNOW, "STARK"? HAHAHAHAHA!
WHAT'S HE LAUGHING ABOUT?
THE SHALLOT KNOWS... AND IT ISN'T ALL THAT FUNNY!
RUB RUB RUB-A-DUB-DUB
WAX
C'MON, BOYS, LESS GABBIN', MORE WAXIN'!
END

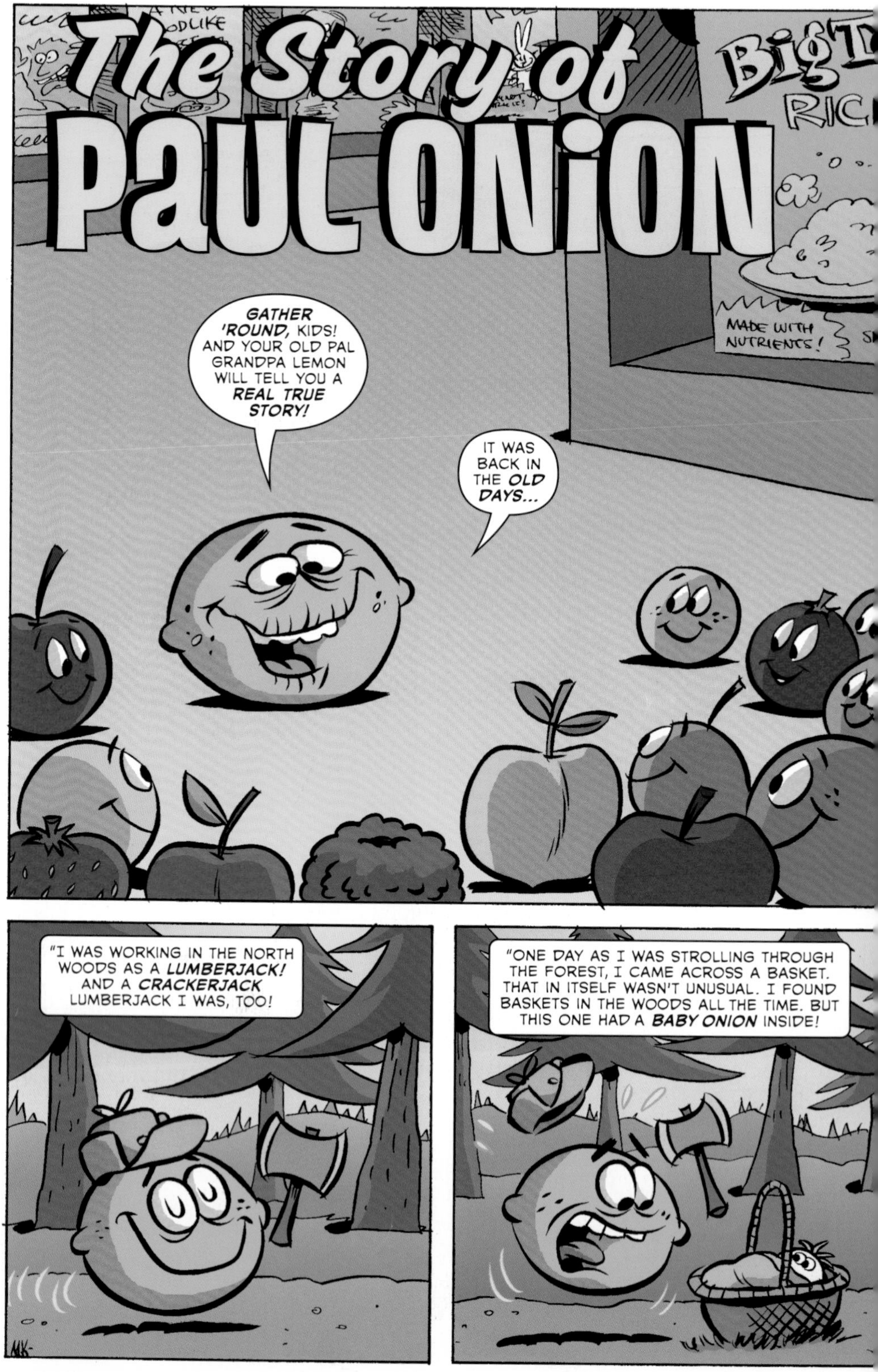
The Story of
PAUL ONION
MADE WITH NUTRIENTS!
GATHER 'ROUND, KIDS! AND YOUR OLD PAL GRANDPA LEMON WILL TELL YOU A REAL TRUE STORY!
IT WAS BACK IN THE OLD DAYS...
"I WAS WORKING IN THE NORTH WOODS AS A LUMBERJACK! AND A CRACKERJACK LUMBERJACK I WAS, TOO!
"ONE DAY AS I WAS STROLLING THROUGH THE FOREST, I CAME ACROSS A BASKET. THAT IN ITSELF WASN'T UNUSUAL. I FOUND BASKETS IN THE WOODS ALL THE TIME. BUT THIS ONE HAD A BABY ONION INSIDE!

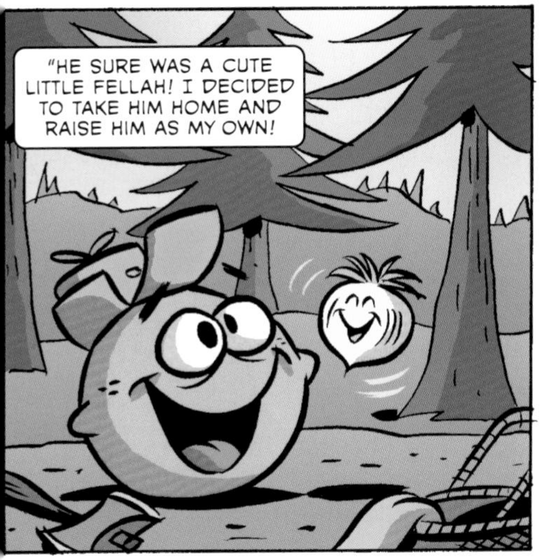
"HE SURE WAS A CUTE LITTLE FELLAH! I DECIDED TO TAKE HIM HOME AND RAISE HIM AS MY OWN!

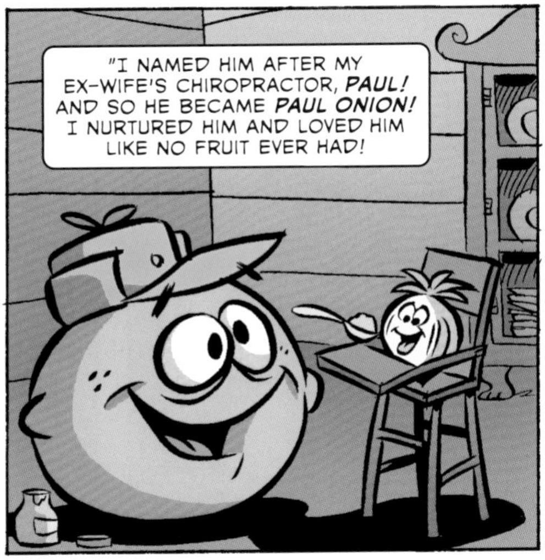
"I NAMED HIM AFTER MY EX-WIFE'S CHIROPRACTOR, PAUL! AND SO HE BECAME PAUL ONION! I NURTURED HIM AND LOVED HIM LIKE NO FRUIT EVER HAD!

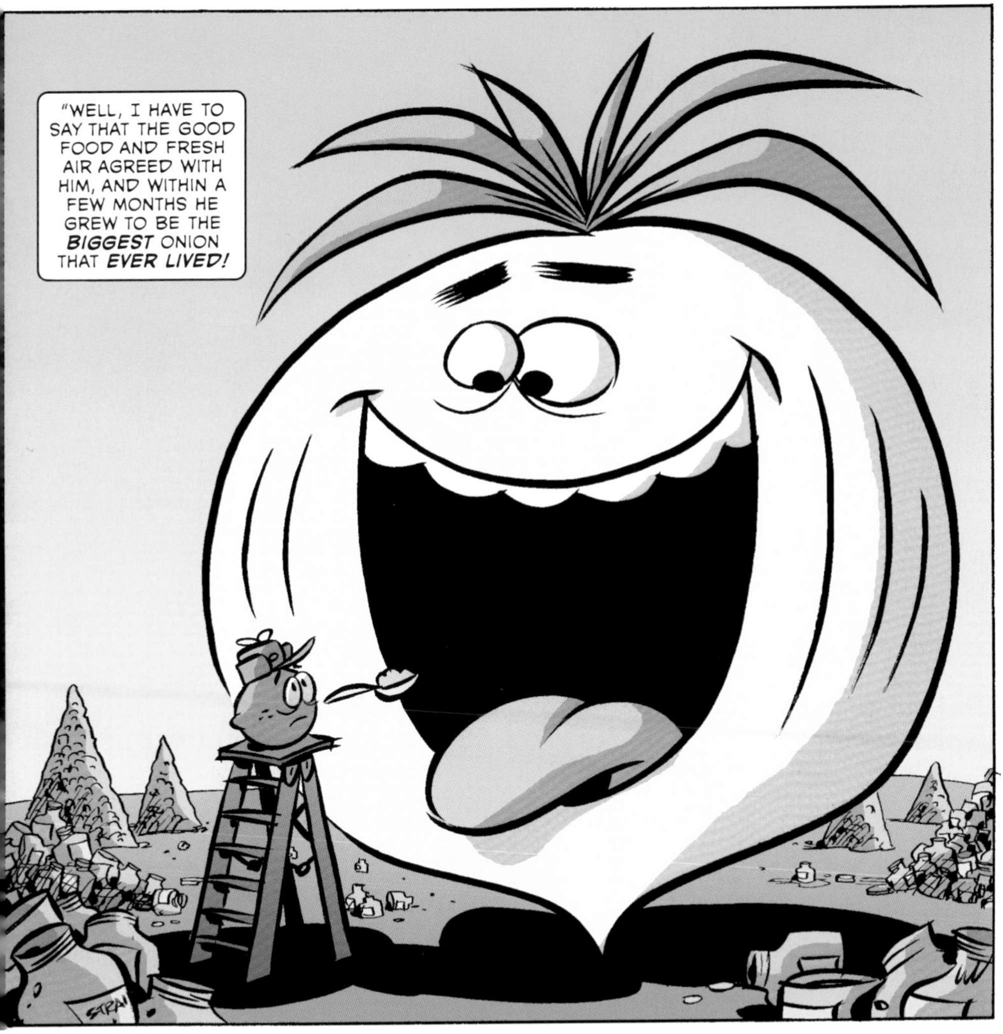
"WELL, I HAVE TO SAY THAT THE GOOD FOOD AND FRESH AIR AGREED WITH HIM, AND WITHIN A FEW MONTHS HE GREW TO BE THE BIGGEST ONION THAT EVER LIVED!

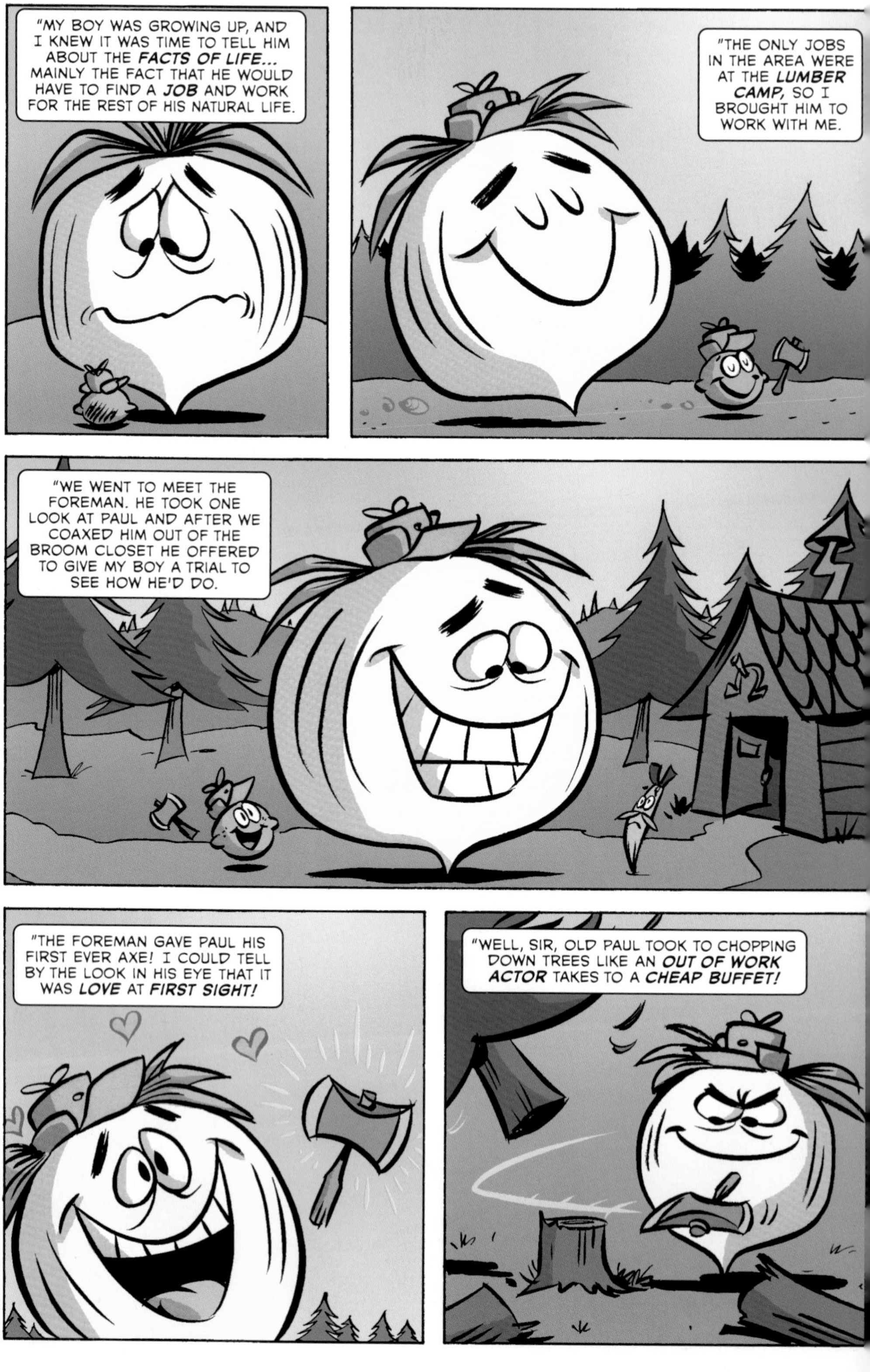
"MY BOY WAS GROWING UP, AND I KNEW IT WAS TIME TO TELL HIM ABOUT THE FACTS OF LIFE... MAINLY THE FACT THAT HE WOULD HAVE TO FIND A JOB AND WORK FOR THE REST OF HIS NATURAL LIFE.
"THE ONLY JOBS IN THE AREA WERE AT THE LUMBER CAMP, SO I BROUGHT HIM TO WORK WITH ME.
"WE WENT TO MEET THE FOREMAN. HE TOOK ONE LOOK AT PAUL AND AFTER WE COAXED HIM OUT OF THE BROOM CLOSET HE OFFERED TO GIVE MY BOY A TRIAL TO SEE HOW HE'D DO.
"THE FOREMAN GAVE PAUL HIS FIRST EVER AXE! I COULD TELL BY THE LOOK IN HIS EYE THAT IT WAS LOVE AT FIRST SIGHT!
"WELL, SIR, OLD PAUL TOOK TO CHOPPING DOWN TREES LIKE AN OUT OF WORK ACTOR TAKES TO A CHEAP BUFFET!

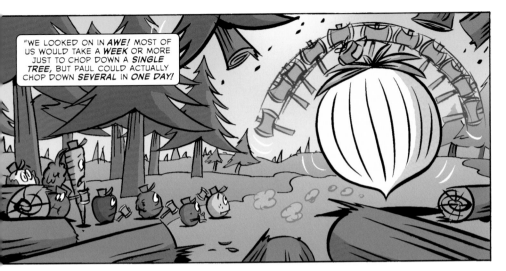

"WE LOOKED ON IN *AWE!* MOST OF US WOULD TAKE A *WEEK* OR MORE JUST TO CHOP DOWN A *SINGLE TREE,* BUT PAUL COULD ACTUALLY CHOP DOWN *SEVERAL* IN *ONE DAY!*

"THE FOREMAN WAS IMPRESSED! HE SAID, 'I HAVEN'T SEEN ANYTHING LIKE IT SINCE WE HAD THAT FIVE-FOOT-EIGHT-INCH *PINEAPPLE* BACK IN EIGHTEEN-AUGHT-NINETY! AND THAT ONION CAN CHOP *RINGS* AROUND HIM!'

"AFTER A WHILE, PAUL BECAME THE BEST LOVED LUMBERJACK IN THE CAMP! I WAS MIGHTY PROUD OF MY BOY! *MIGHTY* PROUD!

"ONE AFTERNOON, PAUL SAID THAT HE WAS GOING OUT FOR A LITTLE WALK. I WATCHED AS HE WENT DOWN THE DIRT PATH INTO THE DEEP WOODS.

49

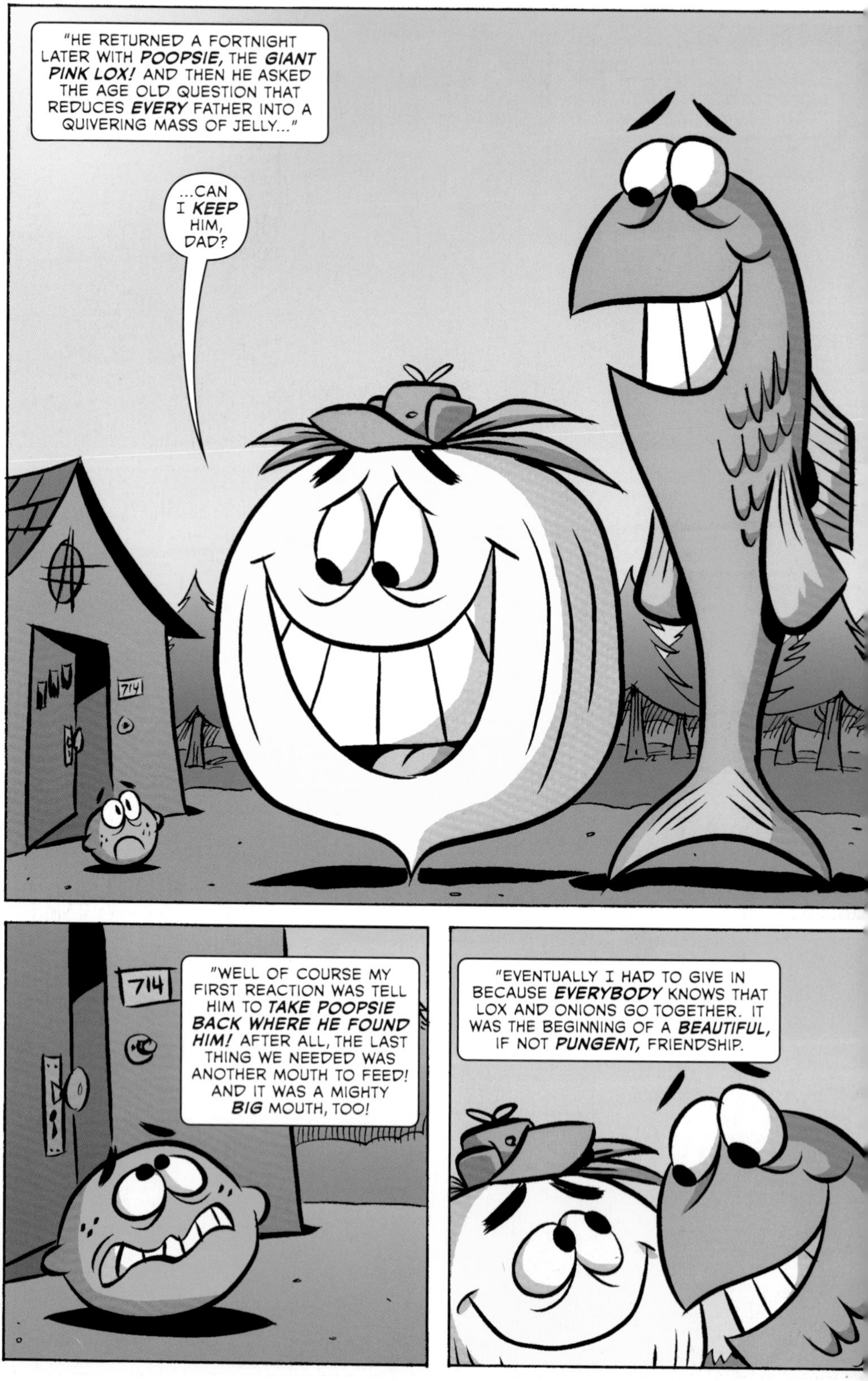
"HE RETURNED A FORTNIGHT LATER WITH POOPSIE, THE GIANT PINK LOX! AND THEN HE ASKED THE AGE OLD QUESTION THAT REDUCES EVERY FATHER INTO A QUIVERING MASS OF JELLY..."
...CAN I KEEP HIM, DAD?
714
"WELL OF COURSE MY FIRST REACTION WAS TELL HIM TO TAKE POOPSIE BACK WHERE HE FOUND HIM! AFTER ALL, THE LAST THING WE NEEDED WAS ANOTHER MOUTH TO FEED! AND IT WAS A MIGHTY BIG MOUTH, TOO!
"EVENTUALLY I HAD TO GIVE IN BECAUSE EVERYBODY KNOWS THAT LOX AND ONIONS GO TOGETHER. IT WAS THE BEGINNING OF A BEAUTIFUL, IF NOT PUNGENT, FRIENDSHIP.

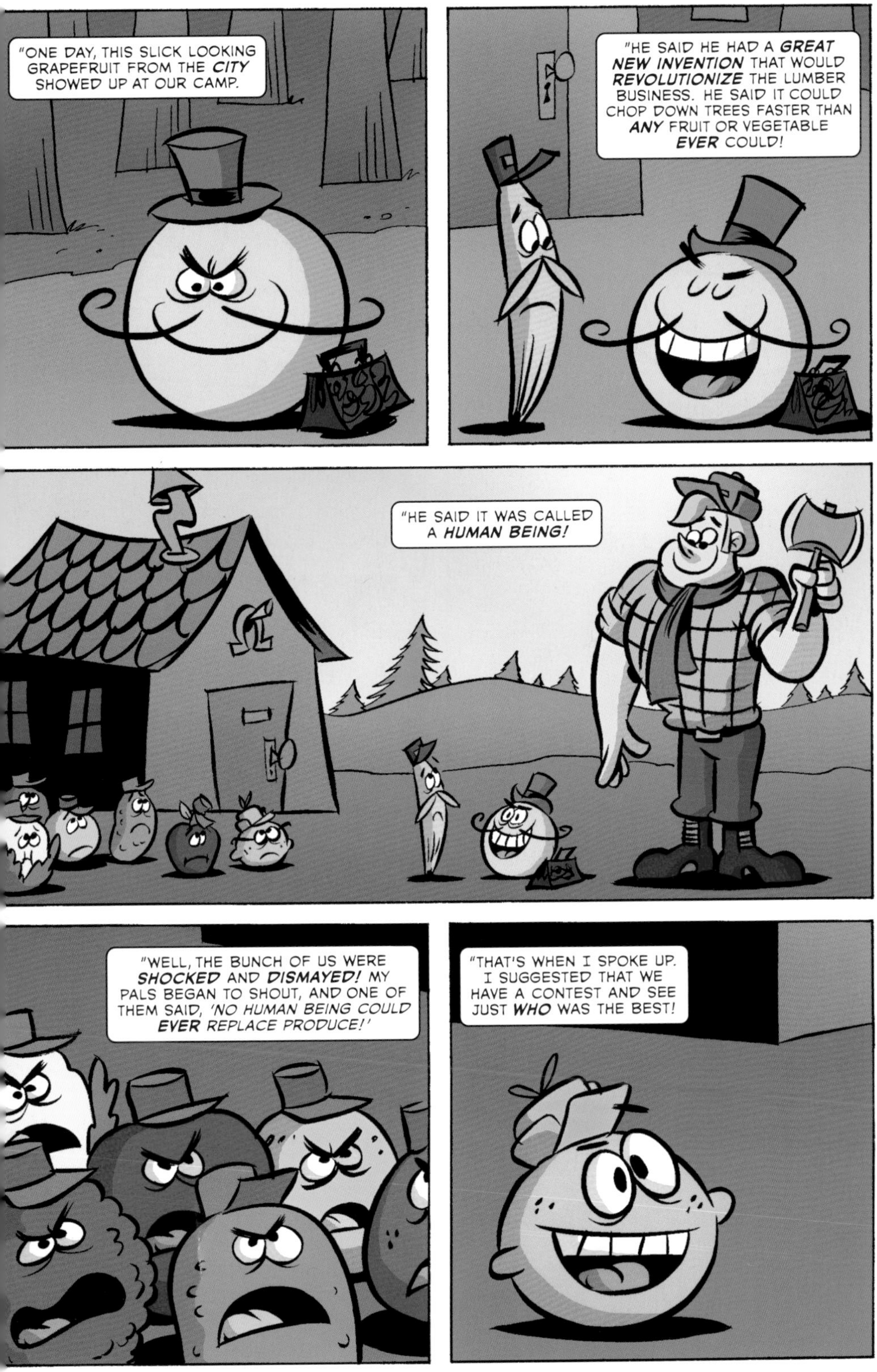
"ONE DAY, THIS SLICK LOOKING GRAPEFRUIT FROM THE *CITY* SHOWED UP AT OUR CAMP.
"HE SAID HE HAD A ***GREAT NEW INVENTION*** THAT WOULD ***REVOLUTIONIZE*** THE LUMBER BUSINESS. HE SAID IT COULD CHOP DOWN TREES FASTER THAN ***ANY*** FRUIT OR VEGETABLE ***EVER*** COULD!
"HE SAID IT WAS CALLED A ***HUMAN BEING!***
"WELL, THE BUNCH OF US WERE ***SHOCKED*** AND ***DISMAYED!*** MY PALS BEGAN TO SHOUT, AND ONE OF THEM SAID, *'NO HUMAN BEING COULD* ***EVER*** *REPLACE PRODUCE!'*
"THAT'S WHEN I SPOKE UP. I SUGGESTED THAT WE HAVE A CONTEST AND SEE JUST ***WHO*** WAS THE BEST!

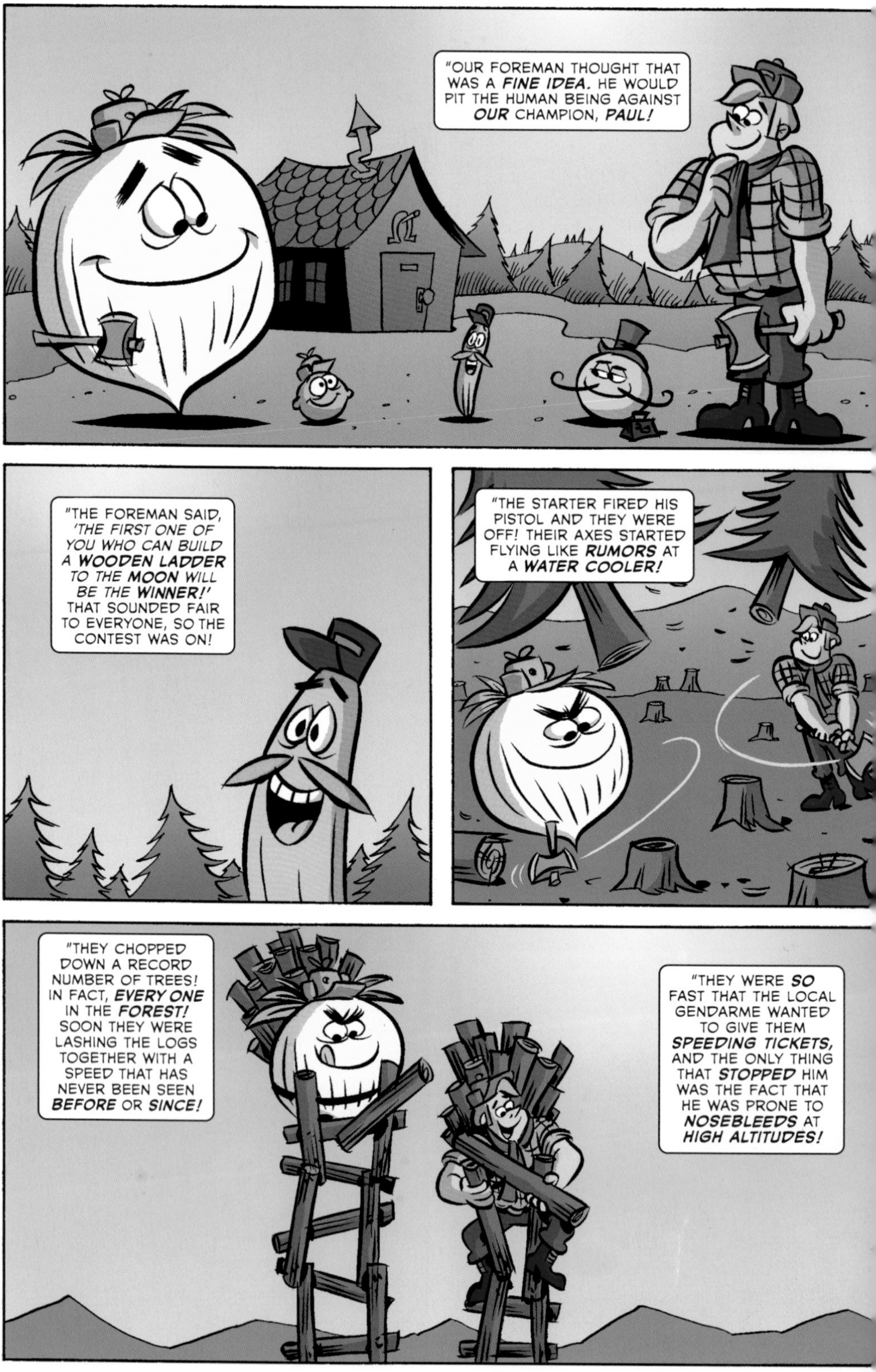
"OUR FOREMAN THOUGHT THAT WAS A FINE IDEA. HE WOULD PIT THE HUMAN BEING AGAINST OUR CHAMPION, PAUL!
"THE FOREMAN SAID, 'THE FIRST ONE OF YOU WHO CAN BUILD A WOODEN LADDER TO THE MOON WILL BE THE WINNER!' THAT SOUNDED FAIR TO EVERYONE, SO THE CONTEST WAS ON!
"THE STARTER FIRED HIS PISTOL AND THEY WERE OFF! THEIR AXES STARTED FLYING LIKE RUMORS AT A WATER COOLER!
"THEY CHOPPED DOWN A RECORD NUMBER OF TREES! IN FACT, EVERY ONE IN THE FOREST! SOON THEY WERE LASHING THE LOGS TOGETHER WITH A SPEED THAT HAS NEVER BEEN SEEN BEFORE OR SINCE!
"THEY WERE SO FAST THAT THE LOCAL GENDARME WANTED TO GIVE THEM SPEEDING TICKETS, AND THE ONLY THING THAT STOPPED HIM WAS THE FACT THAT HE WAS PRONE TO NOSEBLEEDS AT HIGH ALTITUDES!

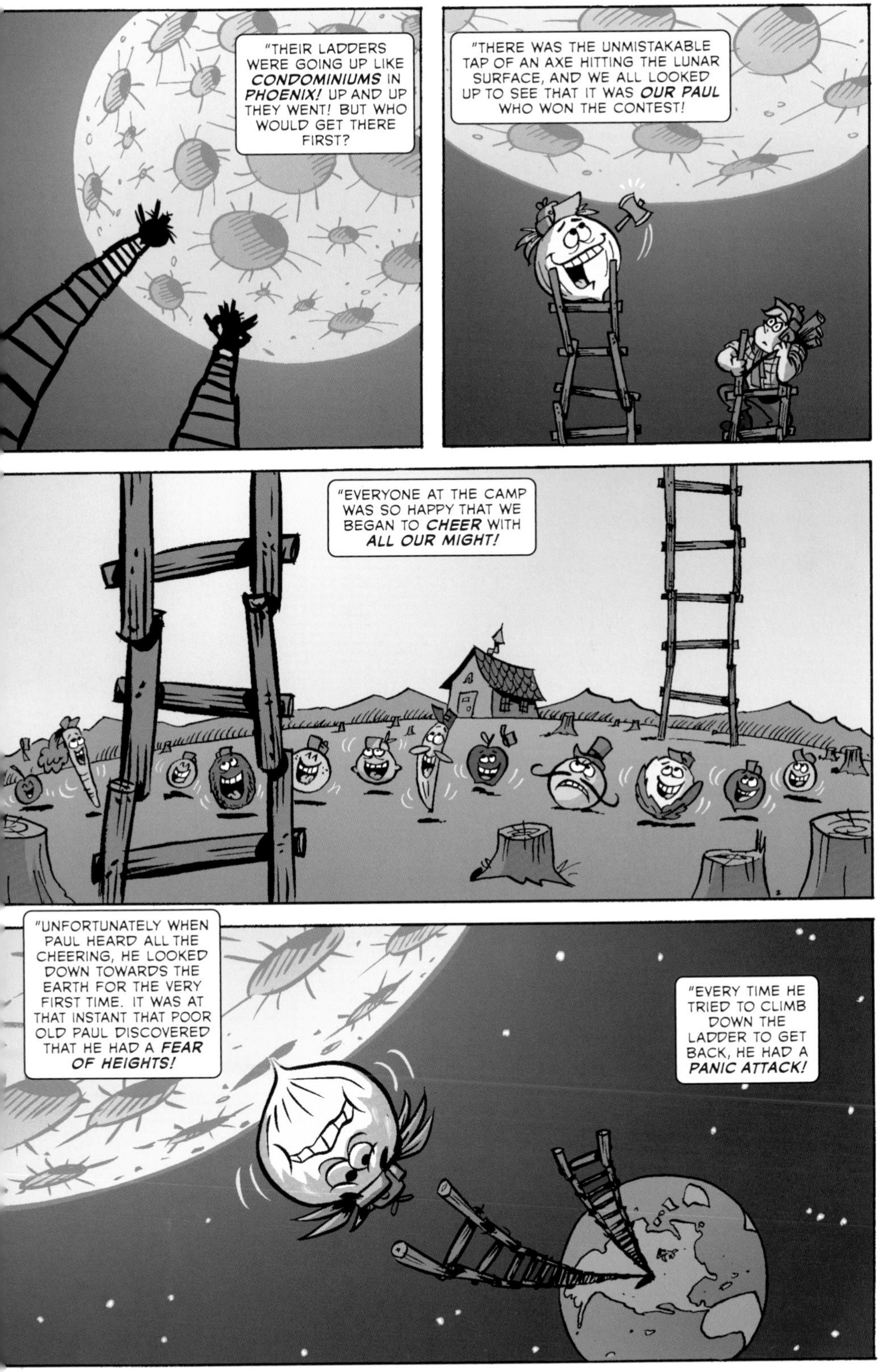
"THEIR LADDERS WERE GOING UP LIKE CONDOMINIUMS IN PHOENIX! UP AND UP THEY WENT! BUT WHO WOULD GET THERE FIRST?
"THERE WAS THE UNMISTAKABLE TAP OF AN AXE HITTING THE LUNAR SURFACE, AND WE ALL LOOKED UP TO SEE THAT IT WAS OUR PAUL WHO WON THE CONTEST!
"EVERYONE AT THE CAMP WAS SO HAPPY THAT WE BEGAN TO CHEER WITH ALL OUR MIGHT!
"UNFORTUNATELY WHEN PAUL HEARD ALL THE CHEERING, HE LOOKED DOWN TOWARDS THE EARTH FOR THE VERY FIRST TIME. IT WAS AT THAT INSTANT THAT POOR OLD PAUL DISCOVERED THAT HE HAD A FEAR OF HEIGHTS!
"EVERY TIME HE TRIED TO CLIMB DOWN THE LADDER TO GET BACK, HE HAD A PANIC ATTACK!

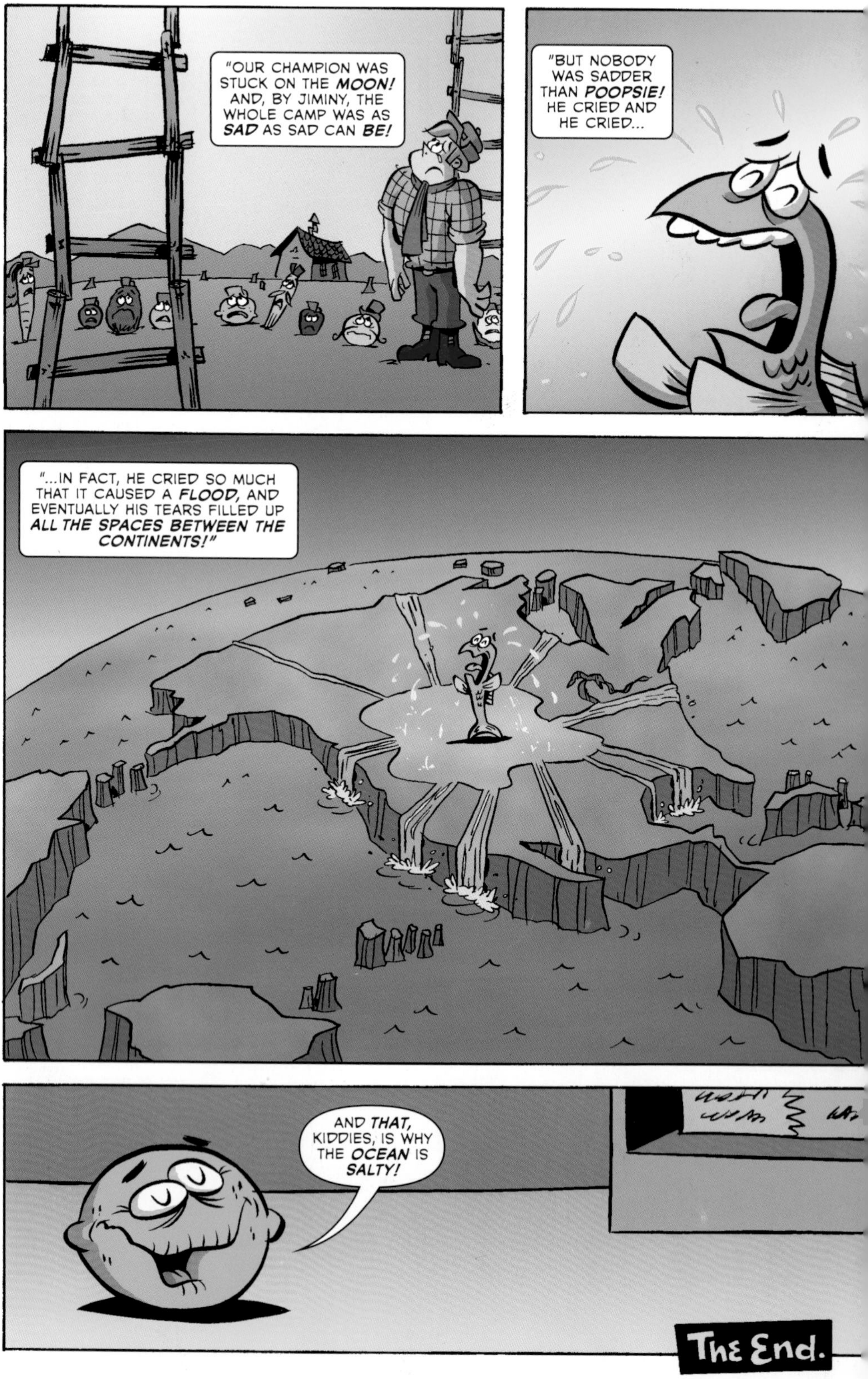
"OUR CHAMPION WAS STUCK ON THE MOON! AND, BY JIMINY, THE WHOLE CAMP WAS AS SAD AS SAD CAN BE!
"BUT NOBODY WAS SADDER THAN POOPSIE! HE CRIED AND HE CRIED...
"...IN FACT, HE CRIED SO MUCH THAT IT CAUSED A FLOOD, AND EVENTUALLY HIS TEARS FILLED UP ALL THE SPACES BETWEEN THE CONTINENTS!"
AND THAT, KIDDIES, IS WHY THE OCEAN IS SALTY!
The End.

ANNOYING ORANGE
IN
WATCH OUT FOR PAPERCUTZ
JIM SALICRUP -- WRITER
(SPECIAL THANKS TO JESSE POST)
MIKE KAZALEH -- ART & COLOR
MICHAEL PETRANEK -- LETTERING
HEY, APPLE! GUESS WHO PAPERCUTZ EDITOR JIM SAUERKRAUT PICKED TO WRITE THE WATCH OUT FOR PAPERCUTZ PAGE?
I DON'T KNOW AND COULDN'T CARE LESS. AND ISN'T THE EDITOR'S NAME JIM SALAD CROP?
DON'T BE SUCH AN APPLE, APPLE! JIM SOURDOUGH ASKED ME TO WRITE THE PAGE!
NOW I CAN TELL MY GAZILLION FANS THE INSIDE STORY OF HOW MY GRAPHIC NOVELS ARE CREATED!
I THOUGHT NERVILLE WROTE AND DREW THEM?
HE'S BEEN A LITTLE DISTRACTED, SO WE BROUGHT IN A COUPLE OF BIG TIME COMICBOOK STARS!
"-- HARDWORKING MIKE KAZALEH AND SCOTT SHAW!"
SNORE
GEE, WITH SUCH TOP-NOTCH TALENT, WHY DO THEY EVEN NEED THAT EDITOR GUY?
WELL, GREAT EDITORS KNOW WHAT TO LEAVE IN AND WHAT TO--
--CUT OUT! YEOW!
SLICE
GUESS PAPER ISN'T THE ONLY THING JIM CUTZ! HAHAHAHAHA!
STAY IN TOUCH!
EMAIL: SALICRUP@PAPERCUTZ.COM
WEB: WWW.PAPERCUTZ.COM
TWITTER: @PAPERCUTZGN
FACEBOOK: PAPERCUTZGRAPHICNOVELS
REGULAR MAIL: PAPERCUTZ, 160 BROADWAY, SUITE 700, EAST WING, NEW YORK, NY 10038

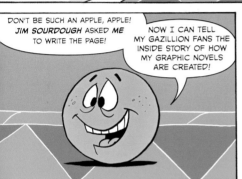

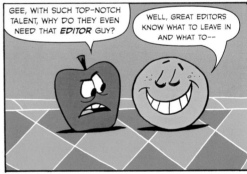

DANE BOEDIGHEIMER

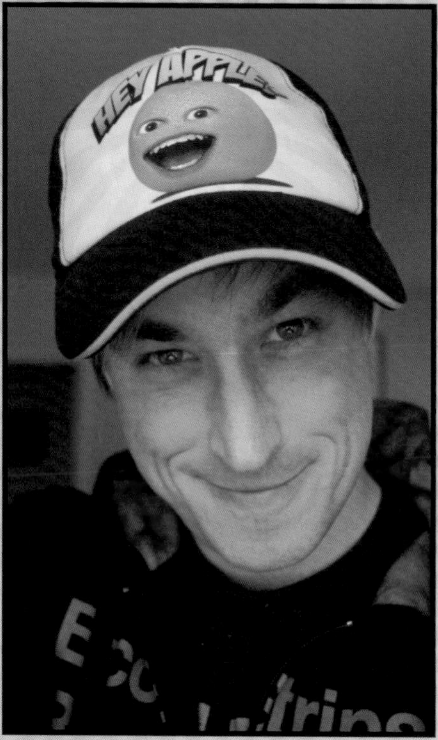
HEY APPLE

Dane (or Daneboe as he's known online) is a filmmaker and goofball extraordinaire. Dane spent most of his life in the glamorous Midwest, Harwood, North Dakota, to be exact. With nothing better to do, (it was North Dakota) at around the age of twelve, Dane began making short movies and videos with his parents' camcorder. Since then he has made hundreds, if not thousands of short web videos… many of which are only funny to him. But Dane has remained determined to make "the perfect short comedy film;" one that will end all social problems and bring laughter to all the children of the world.

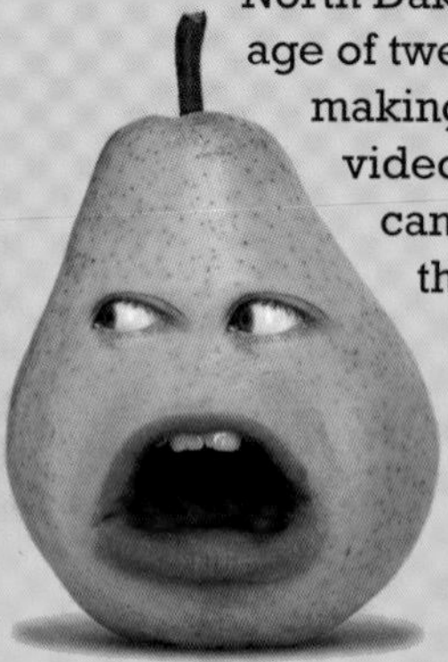

Currently, Dane is most widely known for creating The Annoying Orange, one of the most successful web series ever. The Annoying Orange has over 2 million subscribers and over 1 billion video views on YouTube as well as over 11 million facebook fans. On top of that, The Annoying Orange has a top rated show on Cartoon Network! As a result, fans have clamored for all sorts of cool Annoying Orange toys, t-shirts, games, etc. And despite all the wonderful stuff that has already appeared, fans still want more, and we suspect they'll be getting it.

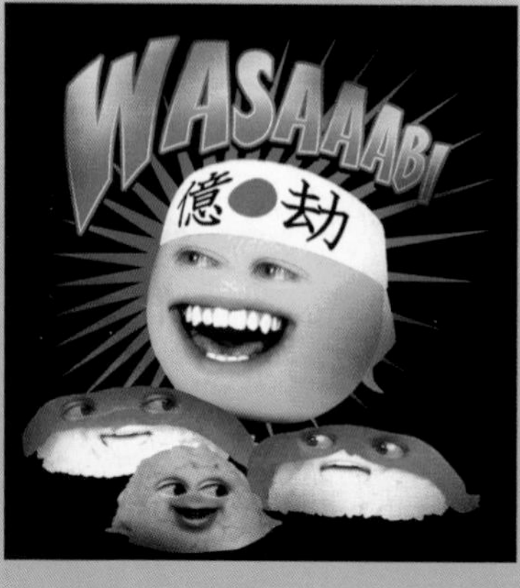
WASAAABI
億劫

Not to be completely undone, Dane's other videos have been viewed over 650 million times and have been featured on TV, as well as some of the most popular entertainment, news, and video sharing sites on the Internet.

In Dane's downtime he enjoys… oh, who are we kidding? Dane doesn't have any downtime. He wouldn't know what to do with himself if he did.

SPENCER GROVE

Spencer Grove has written plays, prose, television scripts and more online videos than any sane person should attempt. Also, he bakes a mean apple pie.

He began his career in independent productions, working on everything from infomercials to award shows, eventually moving to MTV where he served as an Associate Producer on Pimp My Ride. Since 2009, he has served as the head writer of the Annoying Orange web series, creating and co-creating the supporting cast and developing the ever-expanding online world of the Orange.

TOM SHEPPARD

Tom Sheppard is a multiple Emmy-award winning talking animal wordsmith. He's written for all manner of beasts, from genetically altered lab mice, to crazy barnyard animals, butt-obsessed monkeys and even the occasional human, such as the Green Lantern. Since diving into the world of Annoying Orange, it has been his pleasure to expand his repertoire to talking fruit. He is currently writing, producing and directing the live action/animated High Fructose Adventures of Annoying Orange for Cartoon Network.

SCOTT SHAW!

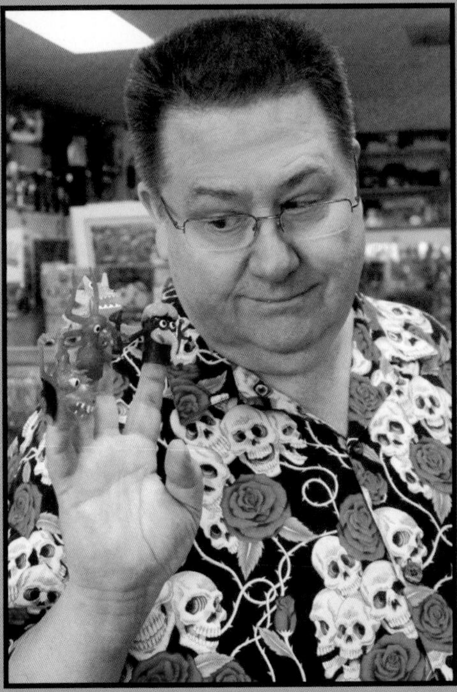

Scott Shaw! is an example of Hunter S. Thompson's statement: "When the going gets weird, the weird turn pro." An award-winning cartoonist/ writer of comicbooks, animation, advertising and toy design, Scott is also a historian of all forms of cartooning. After writing and drawing a number of underground "comix," Scott has worked on many mainstream comicbooks, including: SONIC THE HEDGEHOG (Archie); SIMPSONS COMICS, BART SIMPSON'S TREEHOUSE OF HORROR and RADIOACTIVE MAN (Bongo); WEIRD TALES OF THE RAMONES (Rhino); and his co-creation with Roy Thomas, CAPTAIN CARROT AND HIS AMAZING ZOO CREW! (DC). Scott has also worked on numerous animated cartoons, including: producing/directing of John Candy's Camp Candy (NBC/DIC/Saban) and Martin Short's The Completely Mental Misadventures of Ed Grimley (NBC/ Hanna-Barbera Productions); Garfield and Friends (CBS/Film Roman); and the Emmy-winning Jim Henson's Muppet Babies (CBS/Marvel Productions).

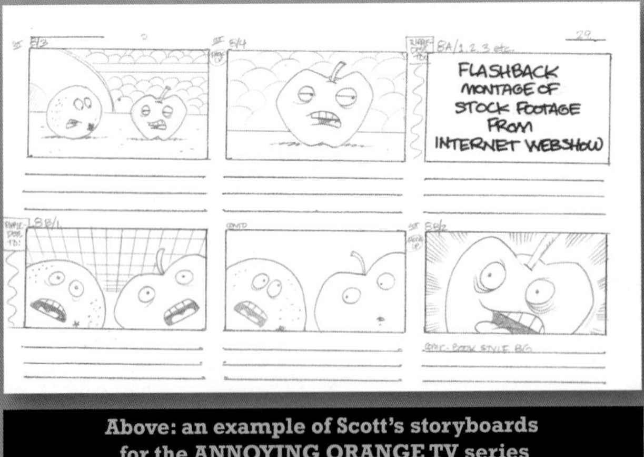
FLASHBACK
MONTAGE OF
STOCK FOOTAGE
FROM
INTERNET WEBSHOW

Above: an example of Scott's storyboards for the ANNOYING ORANGE TV series

As Senior Art Director for the Ogilvy & Mather advertising agency, Scott worked on dozens of commercials for Post Pebbles cereals with the Flintstones. He also designed a line of Hanna-Barbera action figures for McFarlane Toys. Scott was one of the comic fans who organized the first San Diego Comic-Con, where he has become known for performing his hilarious ODDBALL COMICS slide show. shawcartoons.com. Scott is also a gag man and storyboard cartoonist on Cartoon Network's ANNOYING ORANGE program. His favorite fruit is forbidden.

MIKE KAZALEH

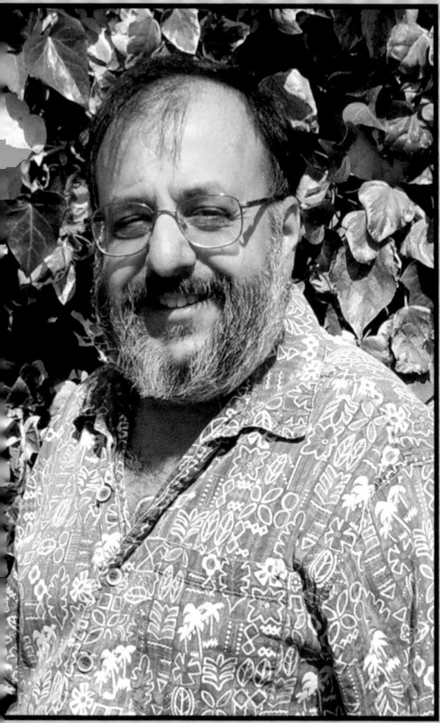

Mike Kazaleh is a veteran of comicbooks and animated cartoons. He began his career producing low budget commercials and sales films out of his tiny studio in Detroit, Michigan. Mike soon moved to Los Angeles, California and since then he has worked for most of the major cartoon studios and comicbook companies.

He has worked with such characters as The Flintstones, The Simpsons, Mighty Mouse, Krypto the Superdog, Ren and Stimpy, Cow and Chicken, and Bugs Bunny, as well as creating his own independent comics including THE ADVENTURES OF CAPTAIN JACK. Before all this stuff happened, Mike was a TV repairman.

Below: A title card designed by Mike Kazaleh.

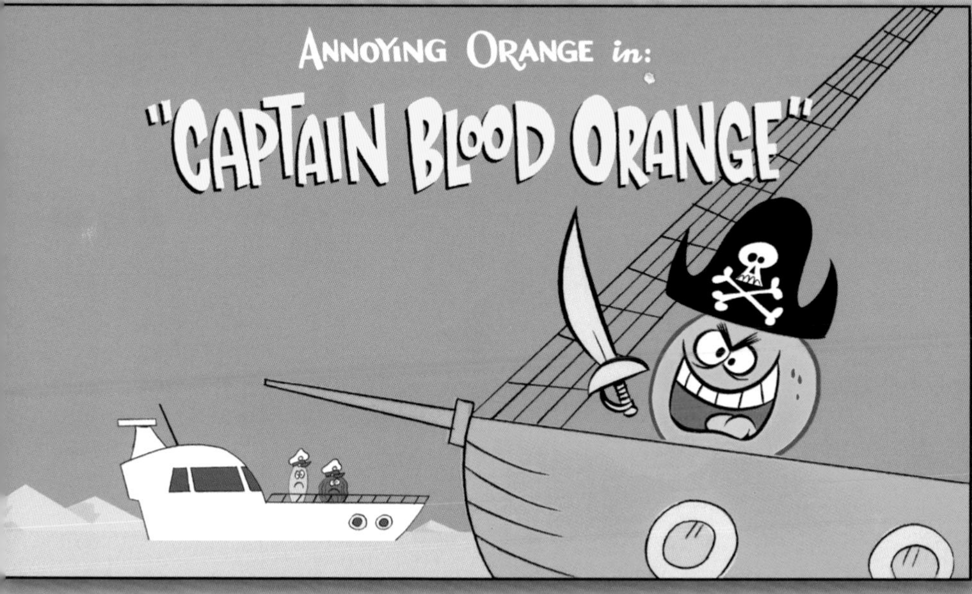
ANNOYING ORANGE in:
"CAPTAIN BLOOD ORANGE"

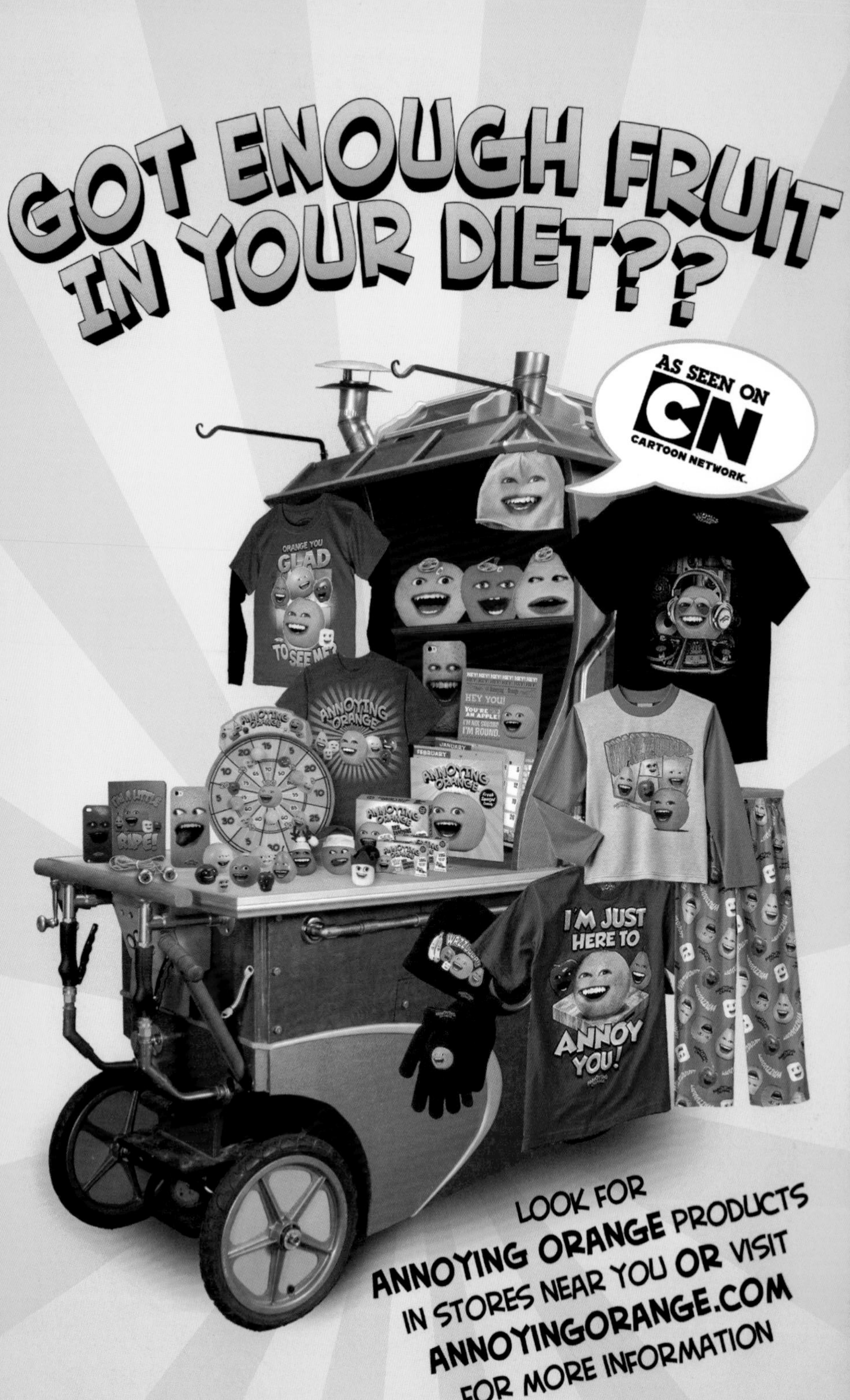
GOT ENOUGH FRUIT IN YOUR DIET??
AS SEEN ON
CN
CARTOON NETWORK
ORANGE YOU GLAD TO SEE ME?
ANNOYING ORANGE
HEY YOU!
I'M ROUND.
ANNOYING ORANGE
I'M JUST HERE TO ANNOY YOU!
LOOK FOR
ANNOYING ORANGE PRODUCTS
IN STORES NEAR YOU OR VISIT
ANNOYINGORANGE.COM
FOR MORE INFORMATION

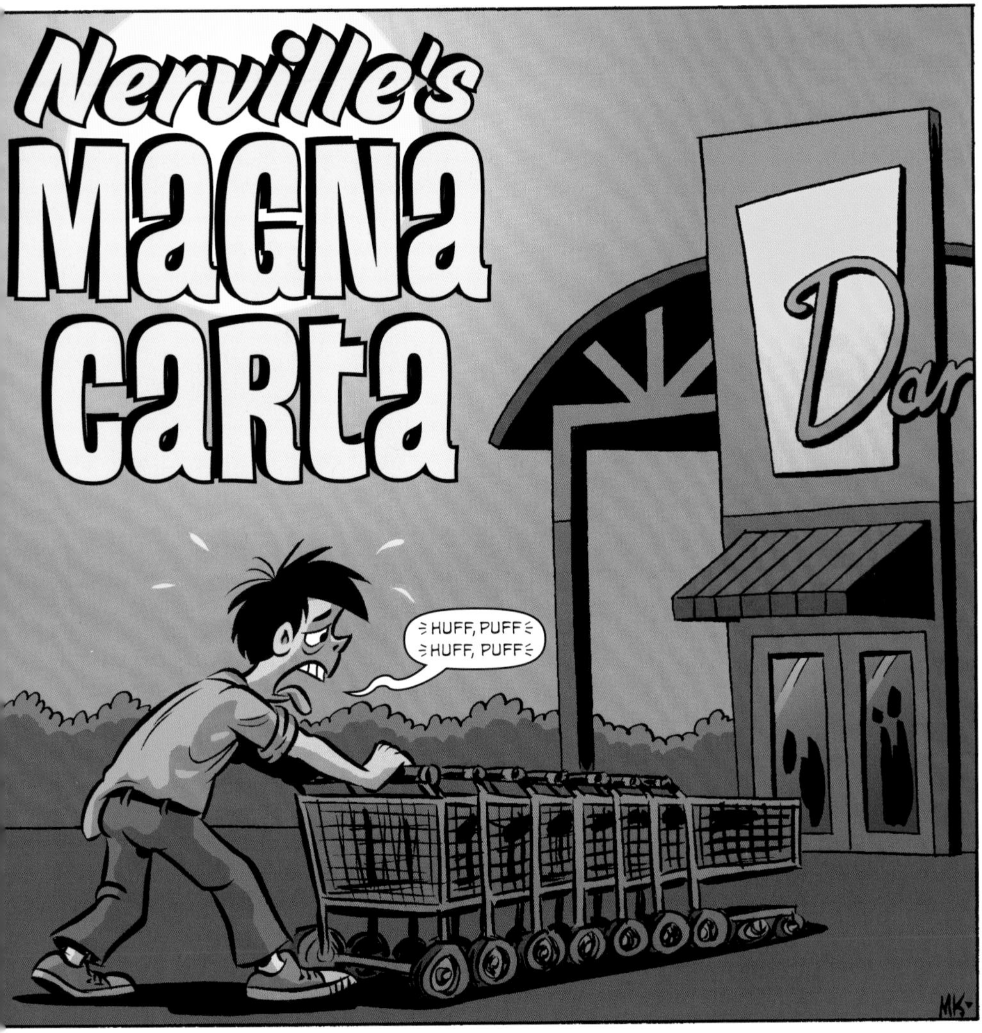
Nerville's
MAGNA
CARTA
HUFF, PUFF
HUFF, PUFF
MK

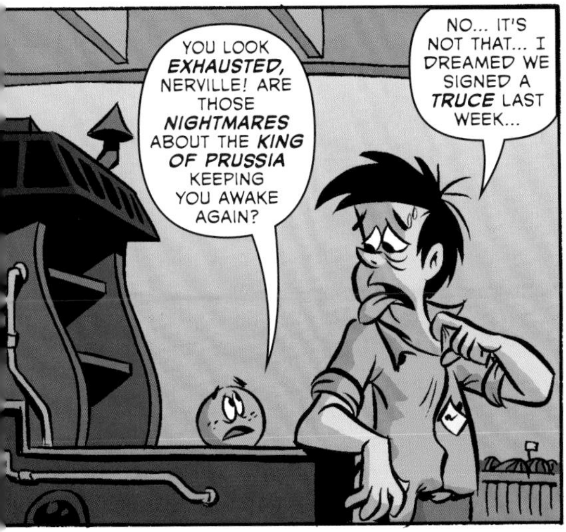
YOU LOOK EXHAUSTED, NERVILLE! ARE THOSE NIGHTMARES ABOUT THE KING OF PRUSSIA KEEPING YOU AWAKE AGAIN?
NO... IT'S NOT THAT... I DREAMED WE SIGNED A TRUCE LAST WEEK...

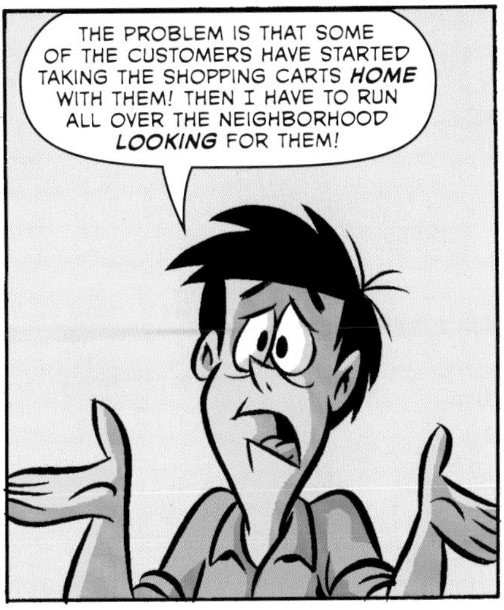
THE PROBLEM IS THAT SOME OF THE CUSTOMERS HAVE STARTED TAKING THE SHOPPING CARTS HOME WITH THEM! THEN I HAVE TO RUN ALL OVER THE NEIGHBORHOOD LOOKING FOR THEM!

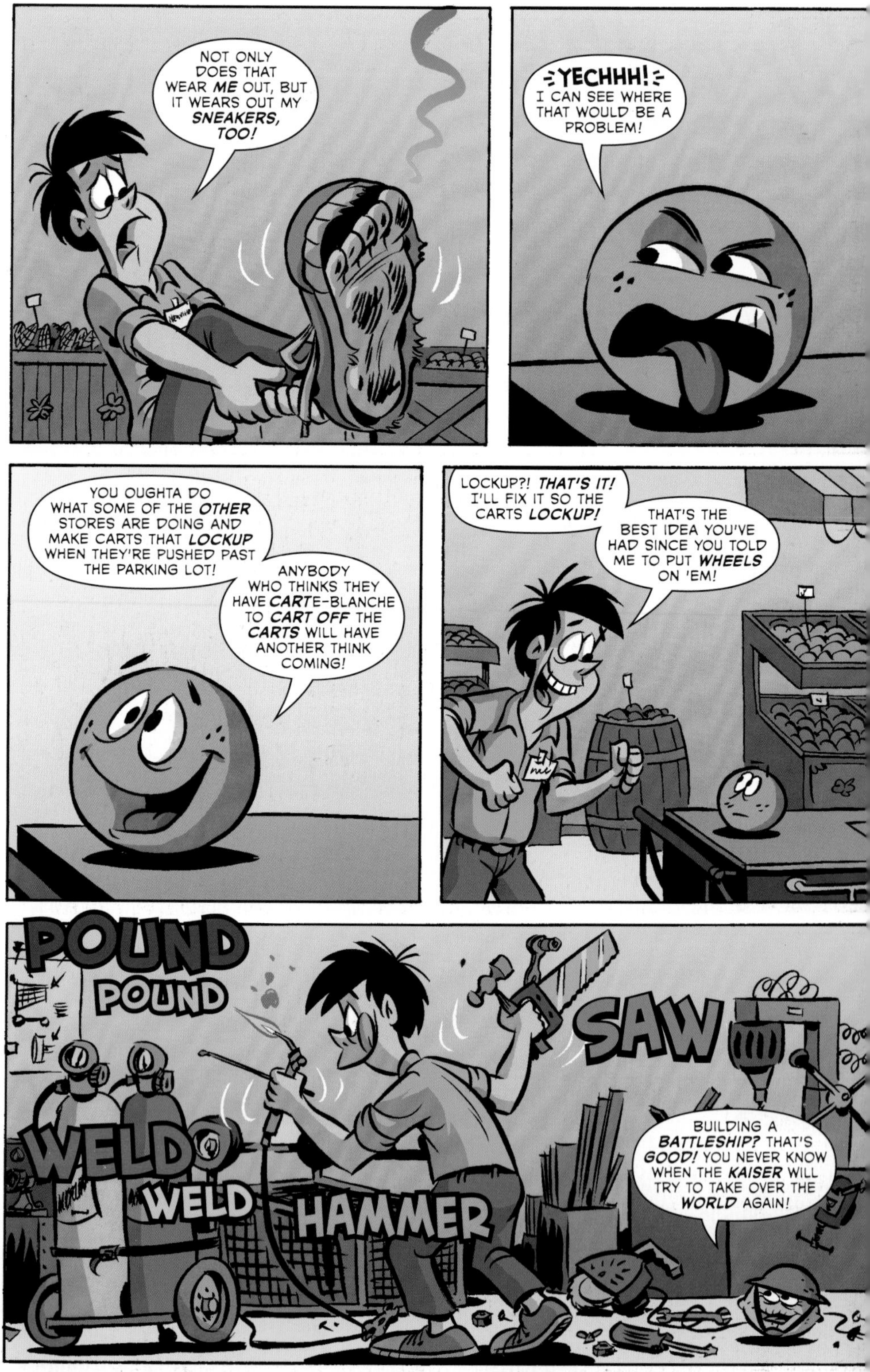
NOT ONLY DOES THAT WEAR ME OUT, BUT IT WEARS OUT MY SNEAKERS, TOO!
YECHHH! I CAN SEE WHERE THAT WOULD BE A PROBLEM!
YOU OUGHTA DO WHAT SOME OF THE OTHER STORES ARE DOING AND MAKE CARTS THAT LOCKUP WHEN THEY'RE PUSHED PAST THE PARKING LOT!
ANYBODY WHO THINKS THEY HAVE CARTE-BLANCHE TO CART OFF THE CARTS WILL HAVE ANOTHER THINK COMING!
LOCKUP?! THAT'S IT! I'LL FIX IT SO THE CARTS LOCKUP!
THAT'S THE BEST IDEA YOU'VE HAD SINCE YOU TOLD ME TO PUT WHEELS ON 'EM!
POUND
POUND
SAW
WELD
WELD
HAMMER
BUILDING A BATTLESHIP? THAT'S GOOD! YOU NEVER KNOW WHEN THE KAISER WILL TRY TO TAKE OVER THE WORLD AGAIN!

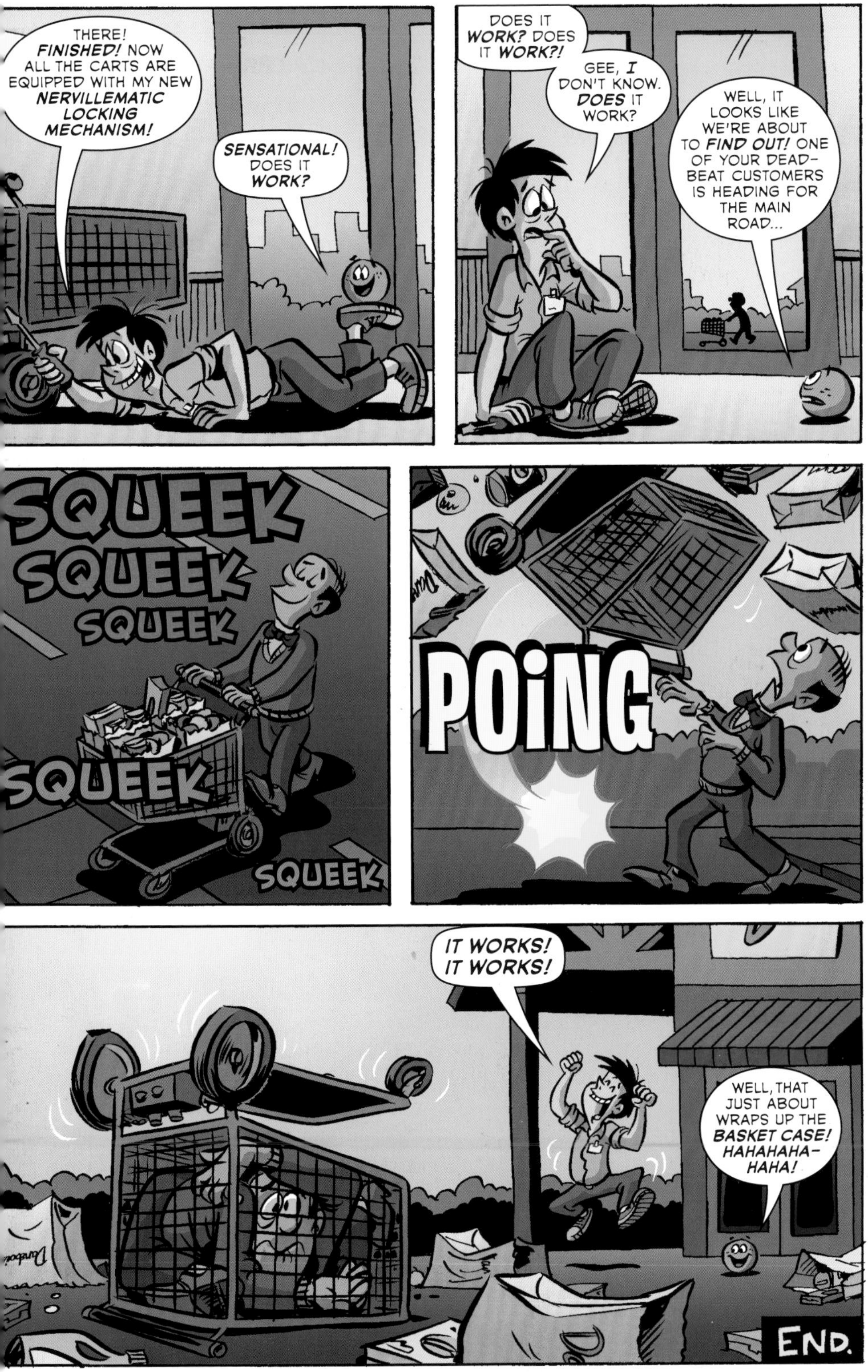
THERE! FINISHED! NOW ALL THE CARTS ARE EQUIPPED WITH MY NEW NERVILLEMATIC LOCKING MECHANISM!
SENSATIONAL! DOES IT WORK?
DOES IT WORK? DOES IT WORK?!
GEE, I DON'T KNOW. DOES IT WORK?
WELL, IT LOOKS LIKE WE'RE ABOUT TO FIND OUT! ONE OF YOUR DEAD-BEAT CUSTOMERS IS HEADING FOR THE MAIN ROAD...
SQUEEK
SQUEEK
SQUEEK
SQUEEK
SQUEEK
POiNG
IT WORKS! IT WORKS!
WELL, THAT JUST ABOUT WRAPS UP THE BASKET CASE! HAHAHAHA-HAHA!
END.

HEY, HEY APPLE!

ORANGE YOU GLAD I'M ON DVD!? HAHA!

AVAILABLE 9.17.13

AVAILABLE NOW

AVAILABLE NOW

THE HIGH FRUCTOSE ADVENTURES OF **ANNOYING ORANGE** VOL. 3: FRUIT WARS

AS SEEN ON **CN** CARTOON NETWORK

FAMILY APPROVED

FEATURING TOBY TURNER AS NERVILLE

THE HIGH FRUCTOSE ADVENTURES OF **ANNOYING ORANGE** VOL. 1: ESCAPE FROM THE KITCHEN

AS SEEN ON **CN** CARTOON NETWORK

THE HIGH FRUCTOSE ADVENTURES OF **ANNOYING ORANGE** VOL. 2: GET JUICED

AS SEEN ON **CN** CARTOON NETWORK

FEATURING TOBY TURNER AS NERVILLE

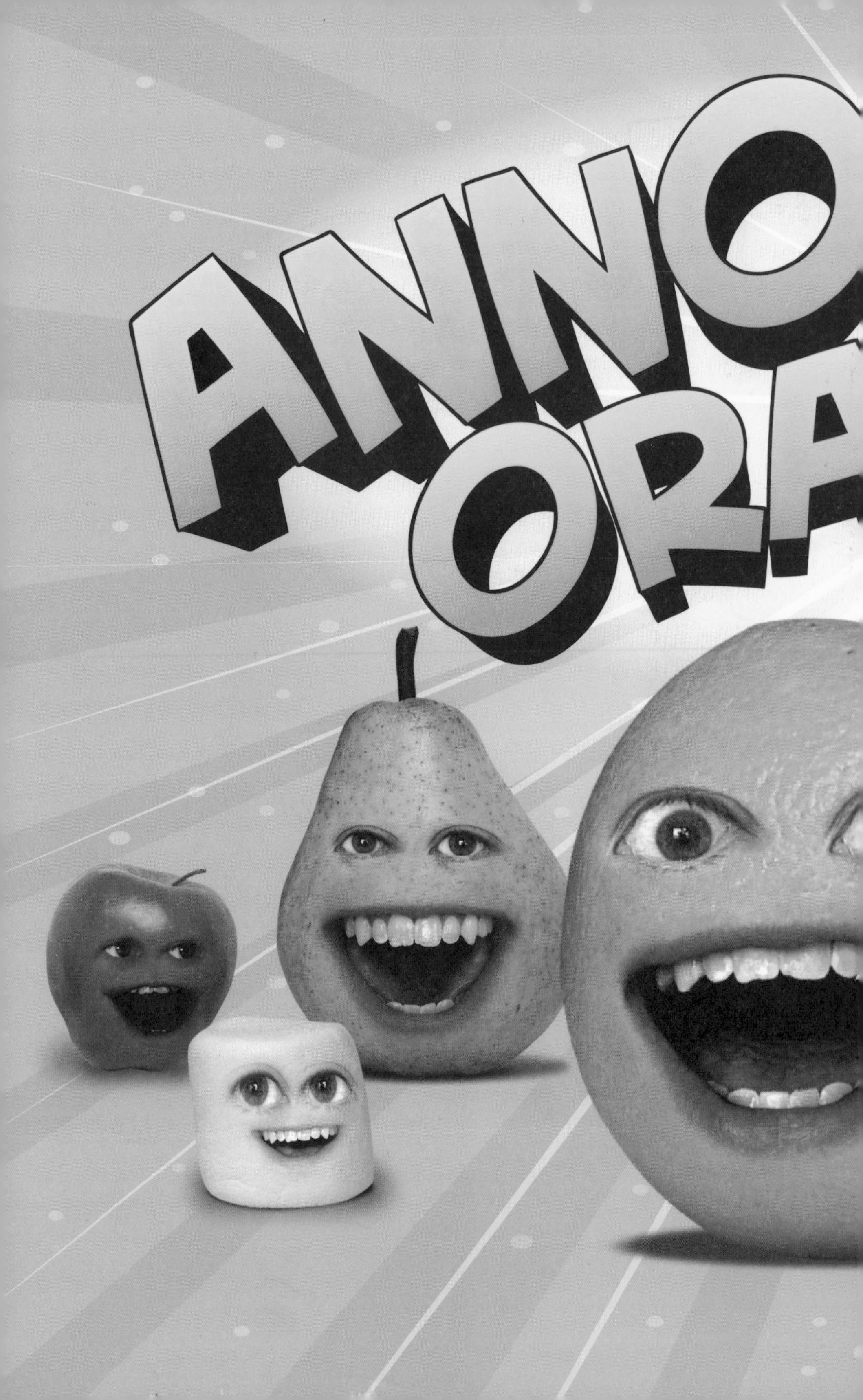
ANNO
ORA